MURDER BY MIDNIGHT

BLYTHE BAKER

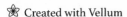

~

When Alice Beckingham boards a train for Edinburgh in 1929, she begins a journey that will test everything she thinks she knows about her past and her family. From the moment of her arrival at the rugged and remote Druiminn Castle, something sinister haunts her steps.

With the murder of her host and the revelation that one of her fellow guests at the castle is an unscrupulous jewel thief, Alice resolves to uncover secrets that someone will stop at nothing to keep hidden.

Coercing the coolly unpredictable Sherborne Sharp into assisting her, Alice follows in the footsteps of her detective cousin Rose and pursues a heartless killer through glittering dining rooms, shadowed passages, and moonlit groves. A mysterious local legend may hold the key to unraveling everything, but will Alice survive long enough to decipher it?

~

1

The afternoon sun poured through the windows but it did little to alleviate the gloom. Darkness gathered in the corners and along the ceiling like thick clouds, and I had to stretch my hands out in front of me to avoid stumbling over the furniture. I knew this house well—it had been our family's country estate since before I was born—but it felt different to me suddenly. More ominous.

Distant voices came to me, growing louder and louder with every step I took towards the door. The door that would lead to the terrace and the expansive lawn beyond. My hands shook, and I tried to call out to someone—my mother or father, my brother or sister, my cousin Rose—but my voice refused to come. I could manage nothing more than dry rasps, my lips forming around mute calls for help.

Then, the double doors to the terrace were thrown open. Sound assaulted me. Cries for help, shouts for a doctor, the moans of a dying man.

The sunlight seemed to pour in all at once, and I turned my head away, throwing an arm over my eyes to shield away some of the brightness. Heat moved through the door, soaking into my clothes and my bones as though the sun itself was just outside the door.

"What is happening?" I asked, finally finding my voice.

No one answered me, so I turned back to the doors. People walked out of the brightness, their silhouettes growing larger and larger until I could see three men holding the body of a fourth. He was draped between them like a rolled up rug, swinging as they walked. I knew immediately the moans were coming from him.

"What is wrong with him?" I asked. I looked around for any sign of my family but they were not there.

The other men laid the injured man on the floor and stepped away.

"Help him," I cried, dropping to my knees beside his still form. "We must send for the doctor."

The noise from moments before had gone quiet, and I could hear my own heartbeat pounding in my ears. When I looked around again, the room was empty. I was alone with the man on the floor. And when I finally looked down, a sob tore out of me.

"Edward," I whispered, reaching out to lay a hand on my brother's chest. "What happened?"

Although I asked the question, I already knew what had happened. He had been shot. Blood burbled from his wound like a stream as I looked for something to staunch the bleeding, even though some part of me was aware it wouldn't help. This was only a dream. Edward was dead and had been so for over two years. Still, I wanted to comfort him.

"Alice," he rasped, reaching out for me.

I grabbed his slippery hand in mine and brought it to my cheek. I felt the wetness of his blood smearing onto my skin, but I didn't care. His face was pale and growing paler by the second. Our time was short, and I had so much I wanted to say. So much I needed to ask him.

"Why did you do it, Edward?" I asked, the words barely coming out between sobs. "You could have stayed with us."

His eyes fluttered closed, and I squeezed his hand, trying to keep him there with me. Trying my best to hold on and not let him slip away.

Edward looked up at me. His mouth opened like he was going to say something, and I leaned forward to hear it, desperate to know what his last words would be. Just as I felt his breath against my face, his hand slipped from mine...

I STARTED AWAKE, breath gasping and pulse racing, to find myself safe in bed, staring up at the familiar ceiling of my bedroom in Ashton House, London.

For a brief moment, I struggled to sort out my confusion as the mists of the dream world gradually receded from my mind, leaving me with cold, stark reality.

I'd grown used to the nightmares. At first, I would wake suddenly, drenched in sweat, and spend the rest of the night pacing around my room waiting for day to break. Over time, however, they became the norm. I had learned how to deal with them, how to put them from my mind.

I pulled the covers up to my neck and rolled onto my side, squeezing my eyes shut. I tried to focus on the softness of my pillow, the warmth of my thick blankets. From the room next to mine, I could hear the gentle sounds of a housemaid moving about, probably opening the drapes and laying the wood for the fireplace. From outside my window drifted the distant sounds of traffic on the streets. The city was never without traffic, no matter how early the hour.

Despite my best efforts, peace and normality eluded me this time.

Even though the nightmare had become routine, it was hard to forget the sight of Edward covered in blood. It was the one thing that still had the power to unmoor me and bring tears stinging at the backs of my eyes.

I did see Edward covered in blood that day in Somerset, but that was not how he had actually died. On that occasion, the doctors saved his life. They patched the gunshot wound in his chest and shipped him off to prison. He had later died behind bars, killed in some random, meaningless brawl with another inmate. I never saw his body then, though, so the image of him bleeding across the carpet of Ridgewick Hall was the memory my mind went to when I thought about Edward's death. After all, he had as good as died that day. He died to our family. We were never all together again. Not until the funeral.

Everything fell apart after Edward went to prison. Our names were in all of the papers as the Beckinghams became known as the family of a criminal. A murderer.

My mother would hardly leave the house. My sister Catherine went pale and quiet, keeping her opinions to herself for the first time in her life. So, I did my best to hold everything together. No one ever talked to me about Edward's death. Not my parents. Or Catherine. My cousin Rose came the closest, but even she didn't want to broach the subject too directly—and could I really blame her? Edward had attempted to make her one of his victims at the end. She'd nearly died by his hands.

Two years had passed by that way. Gradually, our lives had begun to move on, but my nightmares never did...

My busy thoughts and emotions would not allow me to fall back asleep. Giving up the fight, I crawled out of bed, shivering in my nightgown against the chill of the room. I crossed to my window and pushed aside the drapes, letting in the gray light of early morning. Gazing out from this height, I could see the fog shrouded roofs of the neighboring homes, the tops of trees dotting the park across the way, and farther in the distance, the spires of churches and other tall buildings. As I watched, the morning gloom slowly gave way to a brilliant golden sunrise that was almost enough to wash away the memory of my nightmare.

When I walked down to breakfast, I found the meal on the sideboard. There was an assortment of fresh fruit, eggs, toast, and sausage alongside a steaming teapot and a creamer full of milk. I made myself a plate and went to the table to join my father, whose face was characteristically hidden behind the newspaper.

"Good morning, Papa," I sing-songed, holding my teacup with both hands and breathing in the steam.

He lowered the paper and tipped his head to me. It

showed how quiet the house had been in recent months that that barest of acknowledgements made me smile.

The front page of the paper was opened to me, and I noticed the headline: *NYC Museum Proclaims Priceless Painting Pinched.*

"I wonder if Rose will receive a call about the art theft," I mused.

"Huh?" he asked absently.

"On the front page." I reached across the table and tapped the article.

Papa folded back the newspaper to glance at it and then lifted his chin in understanding.

"How far is San Francisco from New York City?" I asked.

"Far," he said. "On the opposite coast."

Rose probably wouldn't get a call, then. I wondered if Rose and her Achilles had solved any robberies in San Francisco yet. My cousin had eloped with the famous private detective some time ago, moving to the United States to open a joint detective agency: Prideaux Investigations. Rose had quietly given up a complicated past and stepped away from a false identity, deciding not to return to her former name of Nellie Dennet or even to keep the identity of Rose Beckingham. Instead, with the blessing of every member of our family, she became Rose Prideaux. The only thing we protested against was the distance she put between us. I missed her terribly.

She wrote frequently, often tucking a secret letter inside an envelope just for me to read, and I responded as quickly as I could. I asked her about married life and what adventures she and her husband had embarked upon. I couldn't help but be jealous every time she wrote to tell me about the exciting cases she had solved. I just wished I had anything even remotely as interesting to write about in return. I told her about the parties I'd attended with my parents and updated her on the state of my French lessons. Rose always claimed she wanted to know everything I was doing, but I couldn't help but wonder whether she found my life pathetic.

"Where is Mama?" I asked, pushing ripe berries around my plate.

"In bed," Papa answered simply. "She was tired this morning. I had the maid take her up a tray."

I rested my chin in my hand. Another quiet breakfast with my thoughts. Another day spent trying to fill my time and keep myself busy.

At the end of breakfast, I picked up the discarded newspaper and scanned the largest articles before flipping to the society pages. There was a ballet in town. The first performance was that night. I was contemplating which of my friends I could convince to attend with me when the dining room door opened.

Our butler, Miller, was standing in the doorway with a bundle of mail in his hand. "Pardon me, Miss Alice. Is Lord Ashton nearby?"

I shook my head. My father had already left the room by that time. "No, but I am. What do you have today? Anything for me?"

"I am sorry, Miss Alice. Not today."

It had only been a week since I'd last sent Rose a letter, so I couldn't be disappointed she hadn't responded yet. I'd also written to Catherine, but I'd long ago given up on any timely correspondence with my sister. She had never been much of a letter writer, even before her marriage two years ago had given her new things to be preoccupied with. After her husband's early retirement, the couple had left New York and settled closer to home in Yorkshire. When I'd visited her there over the previous summer, I'd noticed the way her letters would pile up on the desk in her sitting room before she'd finally sit down to answer them.

Miller stepped away from the door as though he was going to leave, and I quickly called out for him to stay.

I jumped up from my chair, tossing the newspaper aside, and ran around the table, meeting him in the doorway. "I can deliver the mail."

His brow furrowed, creating a crease in the middle of his forehead. "That isn't necessary, Miss. I can see that these letters are delivered to their intended—"

I plucked the bundle of mail from his hand before he could protest further, thanked him for his assistance, and moved up the stairs, shuffling through the letters.

Most of it was for my father. He wrote often to all of his old school friends and to the men he'd met during the war. He was so sullen during meal times that I couldn't imagine him being a very interesting person to receive a letter from, but based on the influx of mail he received every day, I must have been wrong.

Edward's death had distressed Papa most of all. He never discussed it, but after Edward was charged with murder and was later murdered himself, Papa stopped going out as often. He turned down invitations for dinners and dances. I didn't know if he was embarrassed or ashamed or sad. Or, perhaps, all three. He didn't like the attention Edward's actions brought on our family, so he stopped seeking attention in any form at all.

When I shuffled through to the bottom of the stack, I found a thick white envelope addressed in curling script to my mother. I clutched it in my hand and ran up the stairs. When I reached the top, I turned to see Miller still standing in the entryway below, looking as though he didn't know what to do with himself. I waved to him from the landing and then moved down to knock on my mother's door.

"Come in," she called from the other side.

The window had been opened, allowing daylight into the room, but it was still strange to see her lying in bed. Growing up, I had hardly seen her sit down. She was always moving between Edward, Catherine, and me. And when she wasn't devoting her energy to us, she was organizing the day's work with the household staff. But this was now her third morning spent in bed this week.

"How are you feeling?" I asked, closing the door behind me and dropping down on the end of the bed.

Mama pushed her breakfast tray aside and sat up taller. "I'm not ill. Just enjoying a slow morning in bed. Have you seen your father yet?"

I nodded. "We had breakfast together. Or, rather, I had breakfast with the front and back page of the newspaper."

Her mouth tightened. "The morning is when he does his reading for the day. It has always been that way."

I knew she was right, but he had always read the paper while the rest of the family talked. That was fine when there were other people to talk to, but now it was just me. I was tired of seeing the top of his head peeking over the newspaper.

I didn't say any of this, though, and instead held out

the letter to her. "Miller brought this into the dining room for you this morning."

"Oh, it is from Lady Drummond," Mama said, running her fingers over the thick envelope for a moment before tearing away the seal.

I thought I knew all of my mother's friends, but I couldn't recall anyone by that name. My nose wrinkled. "Who is Lady Drummond?"

"I met her at a ball here in town a few months ago. She came in from Scotland to visit family, and we kept one another company during an especially boring party. She has two very strong and handsome sons."

"Her sons were at the ball with you? Why was I not invited?"

"Oh, well," she said, sliding a folded piece of paper out of the envelope. "Her sons were not there, but Lady Drummond is a very attractive woman. And she spoke well of her husband. She did not seem to be the kind of woman who would marry a weak man. Therefore, her sons are likely to be both strong and good looking."

"How could I dare argue with that reasoning?" I teased.

She looked at me over the top of the letter, one eyebrow raised, and then returned her attention to it. She was reading for no more than a few seconds when she yelped in surprise and sat up in bed, lifting herself off of her pillow for, perhaps, the first time all morning.

"What is it? Is everything alright?" I asked

She bid me to be quiet with one hand and continued reading, her eyes scanning the page furiously. When she finished, she dropped the letter in her lap and looked up at me, a wicked smiling twisting her mouth. She looked more like Catherine than I had ever seen before.

"It seems you will be fortunate enough to meet the Drummond men yourself," she said, pointing to the letter. "Lady Drummond has just written to invite us to stay with them in Scotland for a week."

I sighed. "Lady Drummond is your friend, Mama. Perhaps, you should go alone."

"The invitation clearly lists both of us as guests, Alice. It would be rude if I arrived alone."

"Tell them I'm ill," I said. "A plague of some kind."

Her brows lowered, and she shook her head. "You used to be so social. Your father and I discussed chaining you to the dinner table on more than one occasion. Yet now you can't be bothered to make new friends?"

"I have friends," I said. Though, truthfully, I had not seen any of my friends in too long to remember. For a moment, I worried I was more like my father than I wanted to admit. Except, I didn't even have regular correspondence with anyone beyond the members of my own family. Perhaps, I was even worse than him.

"A young lady needs more than friends." The meaning of her words was no secret, and I sagged down, my shoulders hunched to my ears. She moved her foot under the blankets and softly kicked my lower back. "Sit up straight."

"I am not in search of a suitor, Mama."

My mother's eyes went wide. "I'm not even sure I recognize my own daughter. Are you not the same girl who used to promptly fall in love with any young man who so much as smiled in your direction?"

"I was a child then." Still, my cheeks flushed with

embarrassment. If my mother had cared to pay attention to the men I'd chosen to fawn over, she'd have noticed a small pattern—several of them were eventually revealed to be murderers. With a tendency towards that kind of mistake, no one could blame me for being hesitant to make it again.

"And now you are a woman," she said, leaning forward, her hand extended to me. I ignored her for a moment, but then she began to open and close her fingers quickly, asking for my hand, so I turned and gave it to her. She pulled me towards her, forcing me to slide further up the bed so I was sitting next to her hips, and cradled my hand in both of hers. "You have grown into a beautiful young woman who I am very proud of, and who I would be thrilled to introduce to one of my newest friends."

I wanted to refuse her. I didn't want to go and be paraded in front of strange men. I didn't want my mother to be disappointed when I did not end the week smitten and well on my way to an engagement with a Drummond male.

And yet, I couldn't bear to disappoint Mama now. Her eyes were wide, brows pinched together in a question. In the end, I was helpless to do anything other than give her exactly what she wanted.

I rolled my eyes and shrugged, my body slouching forward. "You've convinced me. I will go."

She nudged my back with her hip, urging me to sit up straight, and then clapped her hands together. "This will be so much fun."

2

"Druiminn Castle?" My father looked over the letter from Lady Drummond with a skeptical expression. "For an entire week."

"Will you miss us too much?" Mama smiled, reaching across the gap between their chairs to squeeze his elbow.

Papa didn't smile back. "I'm worried you'll miss home too much," he said, returning the letter to its envelope and setting it on the coffee table. "Rumor says the Drummonds do not live a life of modernity. There is no electricity in the castle. Not even a telephone."

"That sounds like a nice escape from things. Don't you think, Alice?"

I did my best to smile at my mother, but truly, I liked modernity. I wanted more of it, in fact. Catherine always craved our weeks spent in Somerset at the country house, but I had always liked the sound of the city around me. I liked opening my window to hear cars on the streets below, people walking and laughing down the sidewalk at all hours of the night. Briefly living in New York City with my Aunt Sarah in the months after Edward's death had marked one of the best periods in my life—though it followed one of the darkest times. Living in a Scottish castle with strangers for a week without even the luxury of a telephone seemed like more of a punishment than a holiday.

My father's eyes studied me, and I wondered whether he paid enough attention to me to know when I was lying. Or, rather, not telling the whole truth. There was a time when he knew me just as well if not better than anyone. That time had long since passed.

He sighed. "You two are free to do what you will. I know the ladies of my house well enough to know that my counsel counts for very little."

"That isn't true, dear," Mama said. "We value your opinion very highly. But it can't be helped if our own opinions count for more." Once again, she laughed and squeezed his arm.

Papa managed a smile this time, but it did not reach his eyes. He lifted himself out of his chair with a groan and headed towards the door. "I will leave to let you both plan your adventure. I wouldn't want to interrupt anything."

Before either of us could say anything, he left the sitting room and walked across the hall to his study, closing the door behind him.

A look of fleeting disappointment moved across my mother's face before she grabbed the letter from the coffee table and pulled it out to read through it again.

She said, "Lady Drummond mentions that the castle is a little dated, but she told me about it at the ball, and I'm sure we will have a good time."

"Do they live there throughout the rest of the year?" I asked.

She twisted her lips to one side. "I'm not sure. That is something we can ask them when we arrive."

"And when will that be exactly? Our arrival?"

"She invited us to come as soon as we are ready," Mama said excitedly. "I'm sure we can be packed and prepared in only a matter of days."

The surprise must have registered on my face because my mother reached out to pat the back of my hand. "I know you may have had other plans, Alice, but this will be a fun adventure for us girls. Lady Drummond is one of only a few new friends I've met in over two years who has shown any interest in socializing with us."

"But you and Papa are hardly lacking in social activities. You refuse half of the invitations you receive."

"Those are from old friends," she said.

"What is the difference between old friends and new? Is not an invitation still an invitation?"

"For us, perhaps," she said. "But not for you. You came out this past season, and the time to find a young man who could be more than a friend to you is upon us."

I sighed, unable to stop myself. "I've already told you, Mama. I am not interested in—"

She held up a hand to stop me. "That may be true now, and I am not here to change your mind. What I am here to do is make sure when the time does come, you have options. Our family has been through a lot in the past few years and, whether we like it or not, people talk. Gossip has not been kind to us and the number of people willing to forge new friendships with a family who has entertained several murderers, one of them from within our own ranks, is slim. Lady Drummond has been kind to me and is extending that kindness to you, and I will not refuse her."

"So I am to marry one of Lady Drummond's sons or die an old maid? Is that it?"

"You know that is not what I mean."

She was right. I knew I was being stubborn, but Catherine had been much older than me before anyone began talking about her marriage prospects. Why should I be treated differently? Why could I not be allowed the same choice and options as my older sister?"

As if reading my thoughts, my mother began to answer my question. "Our status in society has slipped. The matter was out of our control and it is not your fault or mine, but it is true, nonetheless. Now, in order to regain that status and offer you the same possibilities as Catherine, we cannot be so particular. Lord Drummond is an honorable man and Lady Drummond has welcomed us into their home with open arms despite what she has likely read and heard about us. If we want to dispel the rumors circulating, we cannot hide away at home as though we have something to be ashamed of."

Without meaning to, I glanced across the hall to my father's study door, and my mother's eyes followed. Quickly, she blinked, shook her head, and focused her gaze on me again. "We cannot afford to turn away kindness, so we will be leaving for Druiminn Castle in a few days. I will arrange the entire journey. The only thing I need from you is your beautiful smile and a willing attitude. Can you manage that?"

My mother's speech, though rousing, had done little to spark excitement. However, her expectations of me were low. I was simply expected to appear pleased to have received an invitation and that was something I could do. I stretched a fake smile across my face, and my mother rolled her eyes, though there was a light shining in them.

"That's my girl."

～

ONLY A FEW SHORT DAYS LATER, we found ourselves with our luggage packed and our driver loading it into the car, preparing to take us to the train station.

"Thank you, George," I said, tipping my head as he stowed my trunk in the back.

He smiled, and I wondered that I ever could have been afraid of him. Only a few years before, he was fired from our home after being accused of a crime. He was proven innocent in the end, but at the time, I had nightmares of him sneaking back into our home to kill us. I had replayed memories of being alone with him, wondering if he'd thought of killing me then. Now, of course, I knew those had been the wild imaginings of a child. George had proven himself as harmless as could be and loyal to our family.

I knew my mother hoped for a similar turnaround for our family. She wanted us to be seen amongst good society being sociable, warm, and at ease. She wanted to put the rumors to rest by proving there was nothing less than respectable about the remaining Beckinghams. I understood her desire, but the thought of being locked away in a remote castle for a week with people we barely knew felt ominous.

"Are you sure you won't come with us, Papa?" I asked,

turning to talk to my father who was standing on the steps behind us, a pipe sticking from the corner of his mouth.

He puffed on it, smoke blooming around his face, and nodded. "I'm sure. I plan to catch up on business while the house is quiet."

My mother appeared behind him, laying a hand on his shoulder. "You talk as though Alice and I are often loud. Do we distract you?"

"Only with your beauty." He smiled at her, and my heart pulled.

They had been distant in the last few years. It was understandable, with everything they had endured. My father had never been an especially warm man, but Edward's betrayal seemed to hang like a shadow over every other relationship in Papa's life, as if he no longer fully trusted anyone.

I sometimes wished my sister was still at home to smooth the family tensions. But part of me knew that even if I could have mentioned my concerns to Catherine, she would accuse me of inventing problems where none existed. I'd always been prone to feeling ill at ease prior to tensions or tragedies, but Catherine would scoff at my predictions. The week before Edward was shot and sent to prison, I had complained of a near-constant stomach ache. Though, afterwards, Catherine claimed she couldn't recall my discomfort.

It was Catherine's voice I heard in my head now, when the same kind of ache settled in my stomach at the thought of spending a week at Druiminn Castle.

Do not be silly, Alice. Eating too many sweets does not enable you to sense the future.

I turned away as my parents embraced, my father whispering something to my mother that made her blush. Affectionate moments between them were rare enough that I did not want to ruin this one with my eavesdropping.

When we were finally settled in the backseat, George ready in the driver's position, my father gave one last puff of his pipe and lifted a stationary hand in the air to see us off. Mama blew him a kiss out the window as we drove away, as though we were leaving on a long journey. She didn't sit back properly until my father and the house were out of sight.

"There will be a driver to pick you up when you arrive in Edinburgh, Lady Ashton?" George asked.

"Yes," she said. "The train ride is only a few hours, and the Drummonds will have a car there waiting to deliver us to the castle in the countryside. It is all arranged, so there shouldn't be any problems."

At that very moment, my stomach gave a nervous turn, and I clutched at it.

My mother turned to me, brows pulled together. "Nervous stomach, dear?"

"Perhaps," I said, not wanting to tell her that the bumps of the drive were not upsetting me as much as the thought of our destination was.

"I hope you do not get ill on the train."

I shook my head. "I'm sure it will be fine." I heard Catherine's voice in my head. "Too many pastries over breakfast, I suspect."

"All right, then. No food on the train, though. Just to be safe," she said, a stern finger pointed at me. "I'm sure there will be plenty to eat once we arrive at the castle. I don't want to risk you getting sick on the journey."

I nodded in agreement because I didn't much feel like eating anyway. As the London cityscape sped by and the train station came into view, I focused my energy on beating back the worries trying to claim my attention. Catherine's voice was probably right. I was making trouble out of nothing. My mother and I would have a fine visit and in seven short days, we would be back on this same road headed for home.

I was almost sure of it.

3

Our train ride felt long but was uneventful.

The driver sent by Lady Drummond was waiting for us when we disembarked at the station in Edinburgh, and he drove us silently through the Scottish lowlands.

The sky hung gray and heavy overhead, pressing down on us as though it wished to press us into the ground. Greenery spread out like an ocean as far as the eye could see. Rolling hills broken only by shallow rock faces ebbed and flowed like waves, and despite the premonitions that had preyed on my mind for most of the journey, I couldn't help but be swayed by the splendor of the natural landscape. It was hard to imagine anything ominous could happen while surrounded by so much beauty.

"It is a little dreary today," Mama said, leaning forward to peer up at the sky.

"No drearier than in London," I said. "And the city doesn't have these lovely views."

She turned to me, eyebrows raised nearly to her hairline. "Are you telling me you prefer the countryside to the city? I wish your father were here. He'd sooner faint than believe that."

"I do not prefer it," I said shortly. "But it might not be the worst place to spend a few days of my time."

She pressed her lips together tightly, biting back a smug smile, and I did my best to ignore her. My mother could be a braggart when she was proven right, and I didn't want to spend the entire week with her holding this victory over my head.

Druiminn Castle appeared suddenly, as though conjured from thin air. One moment we were moving through an open bit of the countryside, and the next, we'd crested a hill and Druiminn was lying in a valley beneath us. The driver's only words the entire drive were to confirm that the gray stone building ahead was where we'd be staying for the next week.

As we got closer, I could make out more of the grounds. The raw landscape gave way to structured flower beds and trimmed shrubs. All of the tree branches were clipped back so as not to interfere with the cars driving down the long driveway. When we pulled up in front of the castle, we found that our arrival was anticipated.

The massive steps leading up to the front entrance were flanked by a row of servants dressed in crisp black and white uniforms, standing straight and motionless. A little distance ahead of them was a slender and elegant figure that must have belonged to the lady of the house.

She had on a simple pale green dress that fell well past her knees, the sleeves billowing to her elbows. Bits of shiny ribbon wrapped around her hem, and her shoes—white and green —matched the gown. Her brown hair had flashes of red in it when the light hit it just right, and her smile was as welcoming as any I'd ever seen.

"You must be Alice," she said, stepping forward to reach for me as soon as we stepped out of the car. "Your mother has spoken so highly of you."

I was certain she had, seeing as the reason for this visit was to find out if I would make a fine match for one of Lady Drummond's sons. I said, "I could say the same of you. You have made quite the impression on Mama."

Lady Drummond turned to my mother, her smile spreading even wider. "Eleanor. I am so glad to see you again. When I heard you two would be coming, I could not contain my excitement. Lord Drummond grew quite agitated with me, I fear."

"We are so glad to be here," my mother said, squeezing Lady Drummond's hands and then peering around her to see the castle. "Everything looks so grand. Alice and I were talking on the drive about the beauty of the landscape. Like a picture."

"I am glad we do not disappoint." There was a playful glint in Lady Drummond's eye but it was quickly overshadowed by something else. "I must apologize that the rest of my family are not here to greet you. Everyone is so scattered about the house I could not gather a proper welcoming party."

My mother laughed. "It does not matter. Alice and I are just delighted to find ourselves in such a pleasant setting. We shall be content to meet the rest of our hosts at a later time."

Lady Drummond's expression cleared. "Excellent.

Come now, and let me show you inside," she said, wrapping an arm around my mother's waist and beckoning me. "The servants will bring your things straight up to your rooms."

At the foot of the steps, she paused just long enough to introduce a dignified looking man as the head butler and a female servant in a cap and ruffled apron as the maid who would be looking after us during our stay. I immediately forgot both of their names as we ascended the steps because my mind was overwhelmed by the grandeur of the building that towered over us.

I was accustomed to ancient houses on large country estates, but this one was something special that stood apart from all the rest. My own family's country estate of Ridgewick Hall in Somerset could not compare, either in age or size. Druiminn Castle looked like something out of a medieval storybook. Stone parapets wrapped around the top of towers on each end of the castle and the front doors were immense and painted a bright red that contrasted sharply with the green landscape. I half-expected to see a moat and drawbridge somewhere on the property.

We were nearly up to the red front doors when they suddenly opened and a tall, broad man in a dark brown suit appeared in the doorway.

"Oh," Lady Drummond sighed. "There is my husband. Walter, our guests have arrived."

"I see that," he called back, chuckling to himself. "That is why I've come out to greet them, my beloved."

My mother had been right about Lady Drummond's husband. He was not a weak man at all. Thick and squared at every corner, he would have been imposing had it not been for the constant smile spread across his face. I'd only just met him, but I knew it was constant because of the deep wrinkles around his mouth and eyes. It was obvious he was a joyous man, and I caught myself thinking it wouldn't be bad to be married to a man like that. Perhaps, I could give his sons a chance, after all. Though, just as quickly as the thought entered my mind, I batted it away.

"This is Lady Ashton and her daughter, Alice Beckingham," Lady Drummond said, introducing us.

"Violet has hardly stopped talking of your arrival since we received word," he told us. "She is quite excited to have you both. As am I, of course."

If the exterior of the house looked straight out of a storybook, the inside, despite the rumors, was more modern. It was true there was no electricity, so everything was illuminated with natural daylight and flickering lamps spread strategically around, but it had a cozy feeling I hadn't expected. Rugs covered the stone floors, colorful and plush beneath our feet, and artwork and tapestries covered every wall from floor to ceiling and corner to corner.

"Violet," my mother gasped. "Your home is lovely."

Lady Drummond flushed from the compliment. "Thank you. We do enjoy it. I know many people think we are mad to live in this old place, but I find it charming. It is a piece of history we get to experience every day."

"I think it is magnificent." My mother nudged me. "What do you think, Alice?"

Lady Drummond and her husband turned their attention to me eagerly, and I could see them imagining me in the castle with one of their sons. For that reason, I kept my praise light.

"It is beautiful."

The lady of the house raised her eyebrows slightly and then she smiled.

"How about a tour? Or would you prefer to go up to your rooms and refresh yourselves first? Dinner is still some hours away, but I know how exhausting the journey from London can be. If you would rather change out of your travel clothes and rest until evening –"

"No, no," Mama interrupted. "There will be plenty of time for that later. Right now, we would be much more interested in being shown around your beautiful home, wouldn't we, Alice?"

I nodded in polite agreement and the Drummonds beamed, clearly pleased by our appreciation of their home.

My mother fawned over every room we entered, and I nodded along, signing my name to her compliments, although I couldn't conjure any of my own. My mind was too preoccupied thinking about the reason I was in the castle in the first place.

A few years before, I would have been thrilled at the opportunity to spend a week on holiday and meet a young man in the process. There had been few things I wanted more than to be treated as an adult and for boys to pay attention to me. Now, however, I longed for experience more than adoration. I wanted to be like my cousin Rose who lived all around the world and experienced other places and cultures. I could do without the tragedy that derailed her life, of course, and the year she had to spend secretly assuming someone else's identity. But once the truth came out and she was free to live as Rose, her life was ideal. After a year of excitement and travel, she married Achilles Prideaux—a man who understood her nature and tendencies and even wanted to encourage her curiosity. Could there truly be two such men in existence?

My father and mother had always been happy enough, but theirs was not a relationship I cared to emulate. Lord and Lady Drummond seemed to make a good pair from what little I had seen of them, but I couldn't imagine Lord Drummond would be smiling quite as often if his wife spurned her wifely duties in favor of solving a mystery the way Rose was known to do. And could the Drummond sons stray too far from the temperament of their father? I didn't believe so.

The truth was, I did not know exactly what kind of wife I would be, but I knew I would not be the kind of wife who met guests at the door with a wide smile, armed with shoes that matched my dress and flattering compliments. I would be something else entirely, and I had yet to meet a man who could handle that. Until I did, I had no intention of settling down.

We moved through the sitting room, dining room, and the library, which had a set of double doors that opened onto a stone balcony with exterior steps that delivered us onto a large, flat lawn. Flowers and shrubbery ran the length of the stone walls and framed a walking path that led from the castle to a more modern outbuilding that housed the family's cars. The driver was pulling the car we had arrived in through a large swinging door as Lady Drummond pointed it out to us.

When we walked back into the library, we were met with two new members of the party standing in the middle of the room. I recognized them at once, my stomach dropping at the sight of them.

"Vivian. Charles," my mother said, turning to each in turn, her eyes wide, a smile that looked only slightly forced spreading across her face. "I never would have expected to run into you here."

"Oh, yes," Lady Drummond said. "I invited Mr. and Miss Barry to stay with us, as well. Remember, they were guests at the same London party where you and I met?"

"Now that you mention it, I do recall that," Mama said, only a slight tremor at the corner of her mouth betraying her feelings were anything but pleasure.

Lady Drummond continued, "They arrived only yesterday. I knew you'd be pleased to see one another as I understand your Somerset estates are neighboring and you are all friends."

"Old friends," my mother said quickly, embracing the vibrantly blonde Vivian Barry in a tight hug. "It has been far too long since we have seen one another."

If I hadn't known better, I would have believed Mama's show of joy. However, I knew all too well that neither the Beckinghams nor the Barrys had reason to feel anything but dismay at finding ourselves in one another's company again. Considering the way one tragedy or another seemed to occur every time our two families met, we had formed sort of an unspoken understanding in recent years to avoid running into one another.

Still, I tried to keep my expression neutral. There was no point in betraying to our hosts that this particular surprise was not a welcome one. It was far too late for that.

Vivian's thoughts must have been similar to mine, because she politely hid whatever unease she may have felt at discovering the identities of her fellow guests. She hugged my mother back, looking over her shoulder at me and saying, "Hello, Alice."

I nodded to both of the Barrys, though Charles showed little interest in being overly friendly. Like his sister, he could not be too pleased at this odd coincidence, even if good manners did not allow him to show it.

He was just as blonde as his sister, but where her expression was infused with kindness, his was harder, more serious. I recalled him always being emotional in his youth, but the cynicism was a new development in the last few years. I could scarcely blame him. Everyone who knew the pair of siblings enjoyed their company, but it was hard to discourage the rumors that spread about them. Nothing too sinister, but their lasting singleness sparked curiosity. At one time, they had each shown interest in my own siblings, but clearly that had not gone as planned.

"I have already given you both a tour, but you are more than welcome to join us," Lady Drummond offered.

"Your home is beautiful, and I think I could wander the halls for weeks, but we were just headed out for some fresh air," Vivian said with a smile. "But we will see you all at dinner tonight."

Charles nodded in agreement with his sister and then pointed to a display case affixed to the wall. In it were a series of old weapons, though they were clean and shiny like they had just been purchased. "When Lord Drummond is available, I'd love to learn more about his antique weapon collection."

We had lost Lord Drummond somewhere along the tour, but his wife assured Charles his request could be arranged.

"Charming people," Lady Drummond said when they had gone. "My husband teased me that I made so many friends in London it would be more convenient for us to move there, rather than have them all join us at the castle."

Lady Drummond showed us the kitchen with original stone fireplaces and then led us down a long hall and into a large room with impossibly high ceilings and elaborate stained glass windows set into the back wall.

"This is the ballroom," she said, her voice echoing off the stone. "It was likely used as a chapel at one point in the castle's history."

"It's breathtaking," I said, impressed despite myself.

"It is," agreed a voice from behind me.

I turned to see a young man with the same auburn-colored hair as Lady Drummond and the same square jaw as Lord Drummond looking at me, a clever smile tilting his mouth up in a smile. It was not difficult to guess who he might be.

"Oh, Alastair," Lady Drummond said fondly. "Flirting before you've even been properly introduced."

He extended his hand to me at once, bowing slightly. "Alastair, son of Lady Drummond." Then, he lifted his brows. "You must be Alice."

I accepted his hand, allowing him to squeeze my fingers, but I did not say anything. It was evident from the moment he'd spoken that he had his sights set on winning me, a fact only highlighted by him referring to me as an "it." I refused to play along with his game.

His smile faltered slightly, but before I could take much notice of it, he dropped my hand and turned to my mother. "And Lady Ashton, I have heard a great deal about you."

My mother turned to Lady Drummond. "He is the third person to tell me that, so now I know it must be true."

Lady Drummond laughed. "Alastair is my youngest son. Gordon is my eldest." Her expression seemed to tighten at the mention of her other son, but it smoothed over so quickly as to almost be unnoticeable. "I'm sure you will meet him shortly, as well."

"Wonderful to meet you, Alastair," Mama said, flushing when he kissed the back of her hand. "Your mother spoke kindly of you, as well. She is very proud of you."

"That is because my mother is a saint," Alastair said, beaming at his mother. "We are all lucky she puts up with any of us."

Lady Drummond waved her son away, but it was obvious she was charmed by him. Everyone seemed to be. A young housemaid came into the room while we were talking, and even she brightened at the sight of Alastair, her cheeks going pink when he smiled at her. Yes, he certainly had something about him.

My mother kept glancing over at me, gauging my reaction to him. I did my best to keep my expression neutral, but really, I could think of nothing worse than marrying a charming man.

People always took notice of a charming man. They felt special in his presence and enjoyed the attention he offered. The trouble, however, was that he paid that same attention to everyone. Alastair moved through a room, bestowing praise and smiles on all, so that it was impossible to know whether anyone in particular was special to him or not.

Alastair accompanied us throughout the remainder of the tour, sticking close to my side, though only talking loud enough for the entire party to hear. This suited me just fine because it saved me the trouble of having to speak to him directly, as his mother or mine usually responded to his topic of conversation.

When we returned to the entrance hall, Lord Drummond was standing there with a slim, black-haired young man. The newcomer was dressed in a dark suit and clutched an elegant walking stick. A hat was tucked beneath his arm, as if he'd only just arrived. His handsome features were serene and his bearing confident, yet his overly elaborate costume gave me the immediate impression of a man who liked to exaggerate his standing, possibly because he felt he had something to prove. Maybe he did not feel quite as at ease in this company as he wished to appear?

However, when he turned his dark eyes on us, even across the distance, the boldness and hint of mystery in his gaze made me second guess my initial assessment. There was no lack of assurance in those eyes. For the briefest of moments, I felt my heart flutter, although I could not say why.

The stranger smiled as we walked down the stairs toward him, the expression stretching the narrow black mustache lining his upper lip.

The fluttering sensation I felt ended abruptly when Alastair called down to the stranger.

"Sherborne Sharp," he said, brushing past me to hurry down the stairs. "I wasn't confident you would make it."

The newcomer smiled at him. "I would never miss a chance to mingle with the Drummond clan, my friend." Then, he turned to me, head tilted to the side in mild interest. "Or with your guests."

Lady Drummond introduced us and then wrapped her arm around my mother's elbow, pulling her close, though her voice was loud enough for all of us to hear. "Sherborne is an old school friend of Alastair's. They studied together at Oxford. He is living in London now, but they still keep in touch."

It was unclear whether Lady Drummond approved of their closeness or not, but Lord Drummond's broad smile showed no sign of flagging.

Alastair draped an arm over his friend's shoulder and led him into the sitting room and away from our party, the two of them falling into a lively conversation the rest of us were obviously not meant to be a part of. No one else seemed to find their hasty exit rude, so I pretended not to notice it either.

"Well, that is the tour," Lady Drummond said, moving over to stand with her husband, her arm around his waist. This family seemed incapable of existing without being wrapped around one another in some way or another. "There will be dinner tonight, but outside of meals, we have no planned schedule."

"Just because there is no strict schedule does not mean there are no activities," Lord Drummond added. "There will be shooting parties and picnics, as well as fishing in the hill streams for the gentlemen – and any ladies intrepid enough to attempt it."

My mother tucked her hand around my lower back and pulled me close to her. It appeared the Drummond customs were already wearing off on her. "Intrepid is one of many words you could use to describe my Alice."

She'd said it loudly enough so as to catch the attention of Alastair and his friend through the open doorway of the sitting room, though they quickly returned to their own conversation.

"Perhaps, though I'm not sure I count wading into a cold stream an especially good time," I said with a smile. "I'd much prefer to stay indoors with a book."

"Are you not much for out of doors activities?" Lady Drummond asked. "That would certainly be a shame because we have wonderful stables."

"That was not part of the tour," my mother cried.

"Violet, you were holding out on them," Lord Drummond said, nudging his wife. "Violet adores the stables. She would sleep with the horses if I let her."

"That is hardly true, though I dearly love to ride," she said.

"Alice is quite fond of riding," my mother said. "It is a shame she does not get more opportunity to do it, as we spend so much of our time in the city these days."

"Then she must take every advantage of this opportunity while she is in Scotland," Lady Drummond said, already turning towards the doorway of the sitting room. She raised her voice. "I'm sure Alastair could show her around our stables, if she would like a quick look at our horses."

"What is that you say? Are you making plans for me

already, Mother?" Alastair asked cheerfully, appearing in the doorway.

"No," I said a touch more loudly than necessary. "A tour of the outdoors is not necessary. I am fine."

"You could show Alice to the stables," Lady Drummond said, as though she had not heard me.

Alastair nodded at once. "Of course I can."

I shook my head. "Your friend has only just arrived. I would not like to take you away from Mr. Sharp."

"Sherborne has been to visit us enough times that he knows his way around," Alastair said, waving a dismissive hand towards his friend.

"It's true," Sherborne Sharp put in, appearing at Alastair's side. "Please do not refuse on my account." His dark eyes seemed to dance a little, as if he guessed at my discomfort and it amused him.

I decided then and there that Alastair's friend was not somebody I wished to make a better acquaintance of. I had thought him attractive at first glance, but now I sensed he was the sort of man who enjoyed the embarrassment of others.

Alastair remained insistent. "I'd be happy to show you, Alice," he said.

"Alastair doesn't mind," my mother added quickly, her eyes narrowed on me.

"And I do not mind showing myself," I said, stepping away from the group and moving towards the front door. "Just point in the general direction, and I'll be happy to explore the beautiful grounds."

Alastair and his mother both opened their mouths as though to argue, but before they could, Lord Drummond stepped forward and gestured to his right. "The stables are down this direction. Stick close to the path, and you won't miss them."

"Thank you." I gave him the first genuine smile I'd had since arriving at the castle, bowed my head, and left quickly before Alastair Drummond could be rushed out the door and made to follow me.

4

My mother was exaggerating when she had said how much I enjoyed riding. I was competent enough at it, but it had never been a favorite activity of mine. Catherine, despite her occasionally icy exterior, was more of an animal lover than I ever was.

I was eager to be out of the house, however, to escape the net of matrimony that I could feel both Lady Drummond and my mother attempting to close around me and Alastair. And so, I left the castle behind and followed the dirt path through a thick grove of trees and then exited the foliage to find a wooden building sitting in the middle of a pale green meadow.

The stables looked as though they could have been covered in a kind of fairy magic. Moisture clung in the air, covering every surface in a soft shimmer. When I stepped inside and saw a pure white mare in the first stall, I couldn't help but step closer.

"Hello there," I said softly, not wanting to startle the animal.

She kicked at the ground gently but didn't otherwise seem bothered by my sudden appearance. It was my guess that people were in and out of the stables often.

There was a low wooden stool with a brush resting atop it pushed against the wall, and I walked towards that. "You wouldn't mind if I sat, would you?"

The horse kept eating, which I took as an invitation.

The brush was wooden with coarse bristles and a strap that wrapped around the back of my hand. I picked it up to sit down and it fit naturally around my hand. Then, it seemed silly to wear the brush yet not touch the animal, so tenderly, I reached out and swiped the bristles across her powerful back leg. She shook her head, startling me for a moment, but then she quickly settled, and I stroked her again.

Catherine had talked about the calming effect of horses. How she always felt at peace in their presence. It never made much sense to me until that moment. My time in Druiminn Castle had so far been spent dodging attempts to be partnered up with Alastair. For the first time since my arrival, it felt as though I could take a deep breath.

The air felt sweeter here than in the city. Sweeter, even, than the air in Somerset. It smelled like damp grass and clean hay. I closed my eyes and sighed. "You know, this might be the best time I've had all day. How would you like to spend the next week together?"

I laughed softly to myself, but then a deeper laugh joined mine. The sound came from behind me, and I nearly jumped out of my skin. The brush clattered to the ground, and I slammed back into the stable wall.

"I didn't mean to startle you, Miss." The young man was standing just outside the stall. I couldn't fathom how I hadn't heard him approaching. He leaned against the wooden pillar and crossed his arms over his narrow chest. "I do believe I saw you spending time with my brother only a little while ago. Did he not impress?"

My heart was still racing in my chest, eyes searching for the best path of escape should the situation require it, but I stopped at his words. "Your brother?"

His lips stayed pressed together, but his eyebrow lifted in what could only be amusement, and I saw a flash of familial similarity. His hair was more red than brown, and his face was rounder, more like his mother's.

"You are Gordon Drummond?" I asked, remembering Lady Drummond mentioning his name before.

He didn't answer but instead kept talking. "You might be the first woman not to fall in love with my younger brother on sight. He can hardly smile at a woman without thoughts of marriage entering her head. I'm sure this development will be most upsetting to him."

Usually, I would have held my tongue when discussing a person with a member of their own family, but it was obvious to me that Gordon Drummond was not a man I needed to impress. At the very least, he was not a man I needed to lie to. So, I told him the truth.

"I have no intention of upsetting your brother, but I have no interest in aligning myself with a flatterer," I said, stepping away from the wall and brushing horse hair from the front of my skirt. My cream silk dress was far from the proper attire to wear to a stable, but I'd been eager enough to separate myself from both my mother and Alastair that I hardly noticed.

"A flatterer," Gordon repeated, saying the word like it was his first taste of a fine delicacy. "Do you find him insincere?"

"Incredibly. He flatters everyone he meets, and I am not interested in being one of the many."

Gordon tilted his head to the side and narrowed his eyes. "You are Miss Alice Beckingham?"

I nodded. "I'm sure you've heard my name spoken prior to my arrival. It is my understanding that I am here to be paired with one of the young Drummond men."

"With Alastair," Gordon corrected quickly. "He is the one my mother will want to pair you with."

Gordon was a handsome man, his features more delicate than his brother's or father's, his face and body leaner. I had the impression he could be easily broken, which was perhaps why his expression was so hard. He had to supplement in some way.

"Why not you?" I asked, quickly adding, "Not that I am interested."

He released another laugh, this one sounding more genuine than the first, which despite his protestation, I suspected had been meant to alert me to his presence and startle me. "My mother has long since given up on me, I'm afraid. Alastair is the reason you are here."

"Why?" I asked again.

He sighed like he was already weary with my presence, and I suspected that much in the same way Alastair only charmed people for his own benefit, Gordon only talked to people for his own. As soon as I stopped being a source of amusement for him, he would disappear just as quickly as he'd appeared. The statement I'd made to the horse still stood firm—being alone with her was the best time I'd had all day.

"Alastair does what he is told," Gordon said with no small amount of disdain. "He has always done what he is told, and our parents love him for that. It is why he has shown an interest in you despite possessing none."

I pursed my lips. "I feel I should be insulted."

Gordon's mouth quirked up in a smirk that made him look remarkably like his brother. "I thought you did not like to associate with flatterers. If I was wrong, then forgive me, but I thought you would want to know the truth."

He caught me there. I had no interest in Alastair, so I shouldn't be surprised to hear that he also had none in me. From the moment I'd met him, I recognized his attentions for what they were—staged and pre-planned —so it shouldn't wound my pride to hear those thoughts confirmed.

The horse whinnied behind me, making me jump again, and I rushed forward out of the stall.

"Never turn your back on an animal bigger than you," Gordon said, closing the wooden gate behind me and shutting the mare inside.

"What about people?" I asked. "Does the same hold true with them?"

Gordon turned and, ignoring his own advice, pressed his back against the stall gate, the horse stamping its feet behind him. "In my experience, you shouldn't turn your back on anyone, regardless of size."

I walked down the length of the stable, looking in at a dappled gray horse in the next stall over and a pig with her nursing piglets in the next. Being so far from London and so near to a castle gave me the feeling of being in another time.

"So, I am meant for Alastair," I said, turning to face Gordon again. He was in the same position as before, his eyes still trained on me as though he expected me to lash out and cause some kind of mischief. "Who here is meant for you? Vivian and Charles Barry have been here since yesterday. Does your mother intend Vivian for you?"

"Even if she did, it wouldn't change my opinion on the matter," he said. "I have no interest in anyone here, and I will not allow my life to be dictated by my mother's wishes."

"It seems we are in agreement there," I said.

He nodded and then quickly looked over his shoulder to see that the horse had turned in her stall and was chewing on a large bite of hay just behind him. "My mother tried to set me up with many respectable young ladies over the years, but I did not take to it as kindly as Alastair. He would follow my mother's commands off the side of a cliff, I believe."

"Surely not," I said, biting back a laugh.

Gordon shrugged. "Perhaps we can convince her to test the theory. That would make great fun for me."

"It would be great fun to watch your brother walk off a cliff?" I asked, eyes narrowed.

"It would be great fun to watch him walk to the edge," Gordon clarified. "I've been trying to convince him to live his own life for years, and perhaps a brush with death would be the winning argument."

"Perhaps," I agreed. "Or perhaps he would jump, and

your mother would have only you to burden with all of her love and attention."

At that, Gordon threw back his head and laughed. I walked past him to hide my own smile, pleased with myself for making him laugh, despite my vow to pay no attention to men throughout the entire week.

The white mare was now at the front of the stall, her head hanging over the gate, and I reached out and brushed my hand down the length of her nose. Her eyes, wide and brown, were gentle. I decided then that I would spend more time with horses. Maybe next time Catherine came to visit we could go riding together.

Gordon walked away, moving towards the large stable doors, but he stopped before walking out into the overcast day and turned. "Would you like to ride her?"

I hesitated. It was a strange offer, considering the obvious fact that I was not dressed for riding. Moreover, I had only just arrived after a long journey by train. Did he really think I had the energy or inclination to go out riding across unfamiliar terrain on a strange horse?

And yet, there was something calculating in Gordon's eyes that kept me from refusing. A challenge, of sorts. Was he testing me, finding out my limits and weaknesses? What would it mean if I refused on the very natural grounds that I was weary and inappropriately dressed? I sensed that I would lose something in his estimation, though I wasn't quite sure what.

I found myself nodding, my agreement having more than a hint of defiance attached to it.

As Gordon led the mare out of her stall, a groom appeared out of nowhere, running up to assist. Gordon waved the young man away impatiently and proceeded to saddle up the horse himself, saying nothing as he worked expertly. I watched him and decided he was a man more comfortable in the company of animals. Probably because they did not talk back. When he was ready for me, he extended his hand, and I took it.

There was no stool to help me get onto the animal, so there was no choice but to hook my foot in the stirrup and lift myself into the saddle, an awkward exercise in a dress not designed for the purpose. I pressed the crepe silk material down to cover my legs and then grabbed the reins. The horse started moving at once, eager to get out into the fresh air.

Gordon gripped the horse's halter, leading me out into the stable yard and turning the animal toward the open gate.

He said, "You'll find a good trail outside the gate. The horse knows the way home whenever you're ready to head back."

As he released the halter and stepped back, he added as if it were an afterthought, "Would you like me to wait here and help you dismount?"

I gaped at him, having assumed until now that he meant to accompany me. Surely he did not mean to send me out into the fields alone, without offering himself as guide and companion? I was an experienced enough rider that I was perfectly capable of proceeding on my own, of course, but to assume so was extraordinarily rude behavior in a host, especially a gentleman. Hadn't this whole excursion been at his suggestion?

Still, it was obvious he was eager to leave. Anyway, the same stubbornness that had prevented me from backing down from his first challenge prevented me yet again from protesting against this one.

"I will be perfectly all right on my own," I said with forced casualness. "Besides, if I am to refuse your brother, I ought to grow accustomed to taking care of myself."

Gordon laughed, and as the horse cantered away, picking up speed with every second, I heard him call after me. "My brother does not deserve such an interesting bride, anyway."

When I looked back, he was already walking away.

5

After a brief but refreshing ride across the open fields and rolling hills of the eastern part of the estate, I headed home just as the sky was turning red. Despite my inadequate dress for the outing, I had enjoyed the exercise, the rugged scenery, and the feel of the brisk wind against my face.

On my return to the stable yard, I found a groom awaiting my arrival. I wondered if Gordon had told him to keep an eye out for me. Maybe the young master of the house was not quite as thoughtless as I had assumed after all.

Dismounting and leaving my horse in the care of the groom, I made my way out of the stable yard and back toward the house. Although there was no electricity within the castle, the windows were illuminated by the glow of flickering lamps, as I approached.

Slipping quietly inside, I found myself alone in the entrance hall. I hesitated beneath one of the pools of orange light cast by a wall lamp. I was about to go looking for a servant who might point me toward whatever upstairs bedroom had been assigned to me, when I heard something. A hollow echo rang throughout the open portion of the house, probably a gong calling the family and guests down to dinner. It seemed that I had been out longer than I thought and would now have to forgo the opportunity to tidy up after my ride and change into fresh clothing.

Well, there was nothing for it but to go in to dinner as I was. It certainly would not do to be late to the Drummond's table on my first night as a guest in their home. Mama would never let me forget it. I smoothed back a few strands of hair that the wind had whipped about my face and dusted away a stray piece of hay clinging to the hem of my dress.

Heading toward what I thought was the dining room, I became confused and found myself instead in a long gallery, where the walls were broken only by shadowed doorways leading into empty rooms. Portraits of finely dressed ladies and gentlemen, probably ancestors of my hosts, frowned down on me from high up on the walls. A chilly draft crept along the floor, making the flames flicker in the wall lamps to either side of me. The hairs on the back of my neck stood up, as a sense of isolation crept in on me.

It was ridiculous. There was nothing eerie about this place and I was certainly far from alone. I just had to find my way back into a more inhabited part of the house. That was all.

Hearing a sudden whisper of movement behind me, I turned and nearly jumped out of my skin at the sight of a pale apparition only an arm's length away.

"Are you all right, Miss?"

I exhaled, embarrassed to realize that my "pale apparition" was nothing more than a housemaid wearing a white apron.

"I seem to have become lost," I explained sheepishly. "Could you show me the way to the dining room? I imagine I am quite late by now and the others have probably already gathered there."

Whatever the young woman thought of my silliness she kept to herself, as I soon found myself following her retreating back down the lonely corridor and back into the heart of the house.

I must have looked a worse sight than I thought, for a glance at Mama's face as I entered the grand dining room revealed that her cheeks were flushed with embarrassment.

"There's Alice," Lady Drummond said at my arrival. "We were beginning to worry about you, dear. I'm afraid we were forced to begin without you."

There came the noise of many chairs scraping across the floor as all of the gentlemen at the table set aside their napkins and rose to their feet. I hurried to the empty chair Alastair pulled out next to his own and settled into it, before everyone resumed their seats.

"I apologize for my tardiness," I told everyone. "I had a little difficulty finding the dining room and had to be rescued by a maid."

"That is not uncommon among first time guests," Lord Drummond said sympathetically.

There a brief pause in conversation, while a footman stepped forward, allowing me to fill my plate from the silver serving tray in his gloved hands.

When I was finally free to glance up from my plate, I found Sherborne Sharp looking directly at me from across the table. "I trust you enjoyed your visit to the stables, Miss Alice," he said, a mischievous smirk hovering around the corner of his mouth. "Gordon told us he saw you out there."

I flushed, wondering why the man found it necessary to bring up the awkward subject. Clearly, he could see how everyone was maneuvering me and Alastair toward one another and, just as clearly, he found my reluctance regarding his friend amusing.

"Yes, Gordon told the truth," I said, turning toward the eldest Drummond son, who was sitting at the far end of the table away from his family, his mouth full with a bite of chicken. "He was very friendly and helped me select a horse to ride."

"You went riding?" my mother asked, surveying my outfit, her cheeks reddening further. She hid her embarrassment with a laugh. "I'm surprised only because Alice has always preferred city life. Though, it appears, one day in the Scottish countryside has changed that."

"And I'm surprised that Gordon was friendly," Alastair said beside me, looking down the table at his brother from the corner of his eye.

It was obvious he meant it as an insult, but when his mother cleared her throat, Alastair sat up straight and laughed good naturedly. "I'm only teasing my brother. I'm glad he made you feel welcome, Alice. I would be happy to help you select a horse next time."

"Thank you, but I am used to horses and am sure I will have no trouble selecting my own." His smile faltered, and I fought to keep mine from widening.

The table's attentions moved on fairly quickly to a new arrival, who I had only just noticed sitting on the opposite side of my mother.

"While you were gone, we received another guest," Lady Drummond said, seeing my attention on the man. "Alice, this is Samuel Rigby."

I recognized the name at once, though it took me a moment to place it. "The author?"

The man, blond-haired with a thick mustache, smiled and nodded. "Guilty as charged. I am a longtime acquaintance of Lord and Lady Drummond, and I could not refuse their offer of hospitality when I found myself travelling through Scotland again."

"And we are glad you couldn't," Lord Drummond said, smiling around a mouthful of food. "He is going to regale us with stories after dinner. Won't that be enjoyable?"

Everyone nodded excitedly, and I noticed Vivian Barry lean across the table to catch the author's attention. He was her senior by at least ten years, but that didn't seem to dissuade her. She kept his attention throughout the remainder of the dinner, and true to his word, Gordon Drummond didn't show even the slightest hint of jealousy at her clear infatuation. In fact, he hardly looked up from his dinner at all.

More than me, it seemed Alastair was set on wooing my mother. He spoke to her often, leaning around me to see her, and I let him, even though I knew with every word, he was increasing her expectations of me. When the week ended, and I refused to see Alastair any further, she would tell me what a kind young man he was, what a good husband he would make. And she might even be right, but that didn't change my position on the matter. I knew I could not experience the world with a man like Alastair Drummond by my side. I also knew I could not blame my mother for not understanding my resistance. She was only doing what she thought was best. It was just that her plans did not align with mine.

After dinner, the eclectic group of guests and hosts made their way into the sitting room. A roaring fire burned in the fireplace, making the room noticeably warmer than the rest of the house.

"There are extra blankets in each of your rooms," Lady Drummond said. "The castle is cold, but we will do our best to see to it that none of you freeze."

"This chill is why people no longer live in castles," Charles Barry whispered to his sister. She smiled, but shook her head at him, encouraging him to be quiet so they wouldn't offend our gracious hosts.

"People have survived in this castle for centuries," Sherborne Sharp said. "I'm sure we will survive a week."

"Too true," Samuel Rigby said, drawing the room's attention. "Druiminn Castle has been in this very spot for nearly four-hundred years."

"Was it in another spot before this one?" Charles Barry asked.

"Charles," Vivian chastised, elbowing her brother. Then, she turned to the author. "Ignore him, Mr. Rigby. He enjoys teasing others far too much."

Samuel smiled, undisturbed. "The castle was built by Clan Druiminn in the early 16th century. It was intended to be the home of James Druiminn and his wife. James's father, an illustrious nobleman, intended to arrange his son's marriage to a young woman of distant royal blood, hoping to advance the prestige of his own family name. At the last moment, however, the young woman wed a foreigner, a Frenchman, dashing the family's hopes."

"Those blasted French," Lord Drummond said, a fist raised in the air, though his smile was as wide as ever.

"Young James Drummond, however, had never been interested in the lady or her power anyway," Samuel continued. "He did not want royal connections, and he married a common woman under his father's nose, shaming the entire family."

Gordon was sitting near the open window, a blanket wrapped around his shoulders, and he cleared his throat. I thought I saw Alastair glare at him, but I certainly saw Gordon's face split in a smile almost as wide as his father's.

"What happened to James's father?" Lady Drummond asked.

"Exiled," Samuel said simply. "He could not bear that his son's intended had passed him over in favor of another man, and he plotted to kill her to avenge the slight against his family. He didn't make it very far, of course. His plan was caught out immediately and the lady's royal relations exacted a harsh revenge. Only in old age was he finally permitted to return to Scotland and to this castle, where he lived until he died."

"His grandchildren took it over after that, I believe," Lord Drummond said.

"They did." Samuel grinned, clearly excited to have willing participants in his history lesson. "It was never a castle of large political importance, but it was a safe haven for members of Clan Druiminn and protected them during times of unrest."

"Are you a historian, Mr. Rigby?" my mother asked.

"Hardly, Lady Ashton. I am simply a man who loves a good story, and there are many surrounding this particular castle. Probably the best known would be the tale of The Weeping Woman, if you would care to hear that one."

"The Weeping Woman?" I asked, sitting forward in my seat. The fire raged, but it did little to ease the chill in the room. The temperature seemed suddenly to have dropped by a few degrees. "Who is that? Was she a real woman?"

"Some believe so," Samuel Rigby said. "Me? I believe she is nothing more than a story. That is why I looked deeper into the castle's history. A lot of the time, tales of that nature have a foot in truth."

"And did this one?" I asked.

Samuel Rigby smiled mischievously. "Would you care to hear the historical version or the fictional tale?"

"The tale," Vivian said quickly. She flushed when all eyes turned to her, but quickly straightened her shoulders. "I, too, prefer a good story."

"Then, I will not leave a lady disappointed," Samuel said.

Gordon chuckled to himself in the back of the room, but it didn't seem anyone but me paid him any mind. Everyone else was focused on the author. He was sitting just to the right of the fireplace, the side of his face covered in a thin sheen of sweat from the fire, with the rest of us circled around him, bundled up on the large sofa and chairs. Charles Barry sat on a footstool, Sherborne Sharp in an armchair behind him.

Lord and Lady Drummond had invited an unusual

cast of characters into their home, but for the first time, I could see how we all might fit together for the week. Evenings spent gathered around a fire telling tales didn't seem so bad.

Samuel Rigby launched into his story. "The tale begins with a certain young woman of high birth who once inhabited this castle, a lady distantly related to the current Drummonds living here today. This lady's parents were killed when she was young, leaving her the ward of a cruel uncle, who acted as her guardian. Suitors were presented to her—handsome, strong men who came from good families—but she would not have any of them. Her uncle was determined she should marry well but she would settle for nothing less than true love."

"So, she waited forever and died alone. The end," Sherborne interrupted, his tone bored.

"Aren't you a little young to be so cynical?" I asked, annoyed at him for interrupting the story.

He shrugged, showing no sign of any remorse. Gordon turned from his spot at the window to shake his head at all of us, though he winked when his eye landed on me.

"Keep going," Vivian urged, clapping her hands over her knees. "Did she find true love?"

"She did," Samuel said, grinning at his captive audience. "A local young man came to the castle on behalf of his village, petitioning the lady's uncle to spare the poorest families their due taxes. The master of the castle was not moved by his plea, but the master's niece found the young man enchanting."

"It was love?" my mother asked, her eyes alight with the story.

"True love," Samuel confirmed. "There was opposition of course, but it was eventually overcome. The cruel uncle was persuaded to overlook the low birth of the young man and even took him in as a guest at the castle, as plans proceeded for the lady to marry him."

"I feel inclined to remind our guests," Lord Drummond said, gesturing to Vivian and my mother, who were both sitting with contented smiles on their faces, "that this tale is called The Weeping Woman."

Vivian blinked as though she had been in a trance. "I'd almost forgotten."

"Looks like you could all do with a bit more cynicism," Sherborne said. He was sitting further away from the group now, having slipped away to the back of the room near the doors to rest against the wall. The firelight hardly reached him, so he was half-hidden in shadow.

"Unfortunately," Samuel continued, "the wedding never came to be."

"Did the intended groom die?" Vivian asked, trying to guess the ending. "Was he murdered by the uncle, who was only pretending to accept him?"

"He was not." Samuel paused, leaving us in suspense.

I looked around the room and saw that even the household staff had been attracted by the storytelling. A few servants lingered inconspicuously outside the slightly open door, young housemaids in crisp aprons whispering among themselves and peeking in on the gathering. I supposed they did not often get the opportunity for such entertainment.

I turned my attention back to Samuel, curious about the conclusion. His lips pinched together and then he continued. "The wedding did not occur, because shortly before the wedding, the young lady found her intended with another woman and realized that he had been betraying her all along. Not only that, but he had been stealing from her uncle, as well."

Lady Drummond gasped, as though she had never heard the story before, though I suspected she had, and Sherborne laughed.

"What did she do?" Vivian asked.

"Upon realizing he had never loved her, but had only used her loneliness for his own gain, she grew enraged. She put on the white dress she'd intended to wear at their wedding, and then she laid in wait, finally attacking the young man and planting a blade through his heart. Once he was dead, the woman in white, bloodstained and inconsolable, walked to the highest tower in the castle and stepped through a window, falling to her death. Legend says she can still be seen wandering the hallways in her white dress, weeping and lashing out at anyone who might be considered unfaithful."

The room was silent, the only sound that of the wood crackling in the fire and the wind rattling the windows. It was not storming outside, but the afternoon breeze had certainly grown into something more, and it perfectly complemented the eerie tone of the author's story.

"And that happened in this very castle?" Vivian asked Samuel.

The author reached across the space between them and laid a comforting hand on Vivian's shoulder. She appeared to melt at his touch, color spreading into her cheeks. "No, Miss Barry. That was the fictionalized version. I'm afraid the historical version is less interesting. The young woman did exist, but there was no documented romance to speak of. She simply died of illness while out on a walk and was not found for several days due to a snowstorm."

"That tale is not nearly as dramatic," Lady Drummond said, piercing through the somber mood left behind by the story.

"The truth rarely is," Lord Drummond said. "That is why the stories are invented in the first place."

"Hear, hear," Samuel Rigby agreed, raising his empty hand in a toast.

Slowly, the conversation shifted back to the history of the castle, and despite his insistence that he was simply a writer, Samuel Rigby seemed to have an answer for every question that was posed. He knew more about the castle than either of the Drummonds, and on several occasions, they looked to him for an answer.

The evening only grew colder as the night wore on. I found myself shivering from the chill.

"I have a shawl in my room," my mother said when she noticed how cold I was. "If you run up to fetch it, I'll let you borrow it."

"Bribery?" I asked, lifting an eyebrow.

She smiled and nudged me out of my seat. Alastair was too busy engaging in a riotous discussion with Vivian Barry and Samuel Rigby to notice me leaving. Whatever they were discussing, it had Vivian Barry in a fit of giggles that, for reasons I didn't understand, left her brother looking more sullen than usual.

I picked my way through the room carefully, walking around the sofa and past where Gordon Drummond sat staring out the window. I would have assumed he'd get up and leave as soon as possible, but he seemed content to stare out into the night and cast the occasional reproachful glance at the party. Maybe his parents were forcing him to keep company with the guests, though I couldn't imagine them having any sway on his actions. As he'd made perfectly clear in the stable earlier, he would do as he pleased regardless of their wishes. A thought in the far back of my mind flared to life, and I tried to brush it aside, but I couldn't. What if he was staying close by because of me?

He didn't look up as I passed behind his chair, and when I made it to the hallway, I shook my head at myself, embarrassed that I'd considered the possibility for a moment. Not only was it common knowledge that Gordon had no interest in marrying, but I had claimed the same thing to him. So why was I now contemplating his feelings for me? A foolish habit, I decided. One I would break soon enough.

With everyone gathered in the sitting room, the rest of the house was quiet. And since the house did not run on electricity, the Drummonds seemed to only keep certain wings of the castle illuminated at a time. The stairway to the second floor was dimly lit with flickering lamps, but the upstairs hallway was almost entirely dark except for the barely passable light of the moon coming through a single window at the end of the corridor.

I was startled by the stealthy approach of a gently glowing figure coming down the hall, but relaxed as I recognized the starched uniform of a footman, a dark haired young man who was moving about the corridor lighting lamps that began to illuminate the dimness. Relieved to encounter another human on the silent upper floor, I enquired about the situation of my own room and that of my mother.

After the footman gave me directions to the rooms assigned us, I left him behind and continued down the hall, running my hand along the wall to count the doors as I passed them. When I reached the fourth door on the right, I stopped and turned the handle.

It swung open easily, and I took several steps inside before I saw the dark shadow in the center of the room. The window behind the person was open, the night sky framing the intruder in dark blue, and I saw their silhouette shift as they turned to face me. Before I could even muster a scream, a hand wrapped around my arm, pulled me into the room, and slammed the door closed behind me. It latched with a heavy thud.

6

"Don't scream."

The voice stopped my thrashing, but not the pounding of my heart. A warm hand was tight around my wrist, and I wanted to be free. I wanted to run. Still, I recognized that voice.

"Sherborne?"

The man holding me stepped forward and revealed himself to be Alastair's old school friend. My mind worked backwards, and I suddenly realized I didn't remember seeing him in the sitting room as I'd left. I'd been so distracted with thoughts of Gordon that I hadn't noticed. How long had he been in my mother's room? And why?

"Give me a good reason not to scream," I spat. "What are you doing here?"

He had the nerve to chuckle.

I wrenched my arm out of his grip, stumbling backwards.

He closed the distance between us, ensuring it would

be difficult for me to escape, but did not grab me again. "Probably exactly what you think I was doing."

"Are you a thief?" My eyes were adjusting to the darkness, and I could see something glimmering in his other hand. "Were you going through my mother's jewelry?"

"How very observant of you to notice."

"And why shouldn't I alert the whole house?" I asked.

He shrugged. "Because it would bring unnecessary trouble for the both of us. Allow me to return what I've taken, and we won't speak of this again."

I took another step backwards. The door was just behind me. One quick flick of my arm, and I could have my hand on the doorknob. It would only be a matter of opening it and slipping out before Sherborne could grab me. He was a thief, but would he also prove to be a violent man? Maybe even a murderer? Would he rather kill me than face the consequences of his thievery?

"You have failed to explain why that solution benefits me," I said. "You are in my mother's room, touching her belongings. I have done nothing wrong, so it makes no difference to me whether anyone knows what transpired here."

He nodded. "That is the benefit of being above reproach, Miss Alice. I suppose my offer doesn't benefit you at all. Though, it would be incredibly gracious of you to let me go."

"You don't deserve my grace."

"How can you be so sure of that when you don't truly know me?" he asked.

"You have given me good reason not to know you," I said. "I do not associate with thieves."

I had not seen much of Sherborne since first meeting

him earlier in the day, but my mother did mention the possibility of his presence at the castle prior to our arrival. When she first met Lady Drummond in London, Sherborne came up as a topic of conversation in regards to his friendship with Alastair. It was not a relationship Lady Drummond encouraged. Rumors swirled around Alastair—the nature of them exactly, my mother wouldn't say—and Lady Drummond believed her son should keep better company. Having seen Sherborne Sharp at work, I couldn't help but agree.

He took a step away from me, his hands falling to his sides. "I am not surprised a young lady of your fortunate circumstances would think me unworthy of association. Perhaps I am not as polished as the company you are accustomed to. Certainly my life has not been as easy as it would have been, were I born a Beckingham or a Drummond. My family has... struggled. And now, at last, despite the education and the connections others have sacrificed to provide for me, I find myself in difficulties that offer few honorable paths of escape. You may find that a weak excuse, but it is the only one I can offer for why you have found me driven to this position. Believe me, I am humiliated beyond comprehension."

He did not look humiliated. From the moment I'd met Sherborne Sharp, he had looked perfectly at ease with himself, just as he did now.

"Yes, you seem very upset," I said sarcastically.

"The fact that I am not given to overwrought shows of emotion does not mean I am insincere," he said. "I doubt such matters are within your experience or comprehension, but the truth is that I've found myself in trouble with some debt collectors. They are very unpleasant men, and I'm not sure I will survive an altercation with them."

"What is that supposed to mean?" I asked. "That I would not understand your predicament? Do you think I know nothing of debt collectors?"

"You know nothing of hardship," he said in simple explanation. "It is not meant as an insult. Merely an observation. Your family has managed to hold onto their wealth and position in the world, while the fortunes of my family have declined. You have never been desperate enough to do what I have done."

"An honorable man does not use his circumstances as a reason to commit a crime. Especially against a woman," I said. "It is not as though you are starving and you've stolen a loaf of bread. You lost your money in some sort of gamble and now you cannot pay it back. It seems to me the only person you have to blame is yourself."

Even in the darkness, I could see that Sherborne's face was turning red. I was offending him. I knew the safe thing to do would be to calm him down, gain some distance, and run, but I couldn't find the fear necessary for such actions inside of myself. Sherborne Sharp, though larger and more powerful than me, did not frighten me.

"Your accusation may be correct," he said with an air of forced calm. "But perhaps I see your interruption as a sign from God that thievery was a mistake. How can you know that is untrue? It would be a shame if I were punished forever for a crime I only considered but never committed. I ask for the opportunity to correct what I've done and live a better life. If you tell, no one will ever trust me again."

"And they shouldn't."

"I have been trustworthy to this point," he said. "One mistake does not make me a demon. Have you never made a mistake?"

"You expect me to believe this is your first time stealing anything?" His calm demeanor when I'd caught him in the act was enough to tell me that wasn't true. Sherborne had done this before. He had probably been caught before, as well. And just like he was doing now, he had convinced everyone before to keep his secret to themselves, allowing him to carry on sneaking around and thieving from unsuspecting people who called him friend.

And yet, something he had said touched on an inner vulnerability of mine, a weakness he could not possibly have known about. My own brother had been imprisoned for a crime, in his case a far worse one than anything Sherborne had done. And while in prison, he had died violently. Sherborne's comment had been right, I couldn't be entirely sure he did not mean to mend his ways. I could suspect, but how far was I prepared to condemn him on a suspicion?

I stalled for time in which to make up my mind, asking, "Does Alastair know?"

He shook his head. "Do you think his mother would allow me in the castle if she guessed?"

"I asked if Alastair knew," I corrected. "I know his mother doesn't. She already doesn't like you. Finding out you were a thief would certainly have put a stop to your friendship with her son long ago."

His forehead wrinkled at the information that Lady

Drummond didn't care for him, but it couldn't have been news to him. For all of her smiles, Lady Drummond was particularly reserved when it came to Sherborne Sharp. I'd noticed that immediately on meeting the both of them.

"Alastair doesn't know, and I'd like to keep it that way," he said. "He is a good friend of mine, and I don't want to ruin that relationship because of one error."

"If he was a good friend, you wouldn't steal from his family's guests." I had nothing more to say to Sherborne Sharp, and there was nothing else he could say to me to convince me he wasn't a habitual thief. Sensing our conversation was at an end, I turned to leave. This time, Sherborne made no move to stop me. Until we heard footsteps on the stone stairs.

The voices of the other guests carried up the stairway and down the hall. I could hear Lady Drummond explaining the schedule for the next day and Lord Drummond discussing the architecture of the castle with Samuel Rigby. Everyone was coming upstairs for the evening.

Sherborne surely realized that not only was his secret moments away from being revealed, but there would be no opportunity for him to escape. If everyone had stayed in the sitting room, I would have had to go all the way downstairs to tell the Drummonds about the guest they had allowed into their home, giving Sherborne the opportunity to run out the front door. As it was, though, he would be trapped in my mother's room with nowhere to turn.

Suddenly, he reached out and grabbed my arm again.

He did not squeeze hard or jerk me around. It was a soft, pleading touch. "I will leave here first thing in the morning. Before the sun comes up. Do not tell anyone what you saw tonight, and I swear I will leave."

I hesitated, the memory of Edward's face flashing through my mind. It made no sense. This man had nothing in common with my brother, beyond the fact they had both been caught in the middle of a crime. There was no rational reason to allow Sherborne to get away with what he had attempted.

"Please, Alice," Sherborne said, letting go of my wrist. He was begging me at the same time he was letting me go, allowing me to make my choice.

He turned his face towards the window, the right side of him illuminated by the moonlight. If I didn't know what I knew about him, I would almost find him handsome. Now, however, he looked like trouble.

The voices in the hallway grew louder, and I knew I did not have long to decide. If I waited too long, my mother would walk into her room to find the two of us alone together. There were not many explanations for Sherborne to be in my mother's room, let alone in the company of her daughter. So, before I could second guess myself, I grabbed Sherborne's arm, opened the door, and pulled him into the hallway behind me. The moment we stepped into the hall, the party rounded the corner, Lady Drummond in the lead.

"There you two are," she said, eyes narrowed in suspicion. "We missed you."

"I came for my mother's shawl," I explained, though my hands were empty.

"But she ran into me, and I distracted her," Sherborne added quickly. He glanced down at me nervously, wondering how much I would add to his version of events. Would I tell them of his thievery?

I smiled. "He is such good company that I suppose I lost track of time."

My mother pushed her way to the front of the group to stand next to Lady Drummond. They wore matching expressions of suspicion. "I began to wonder whether you were coming back at all," Mama said.

"Sorry. I'm glad to see you didn't freeze without your shawl. That would have been a weight on my conscience."

Sherborne let out a breathy laugh that, knowing what I knew, sounded more relieved than anything else. I was going to keep his secret, and he knew it.

Alastair saw Vivian Barry to her room at the end of the hall and then came to join our group outside my mother's door. "You left in the middle of the story, Sherborne."

"I've heard it before," he said. "We all have. Too many times to count. I've spent many days in this castle since I was a boy, and I've never seen the weeping woman."

"That is because it is only a story," I pointed out coolly.

"Yes." Sherborne nodded. "But there are those among us who claim to have seen her spirit."

I lifted an eyebrow. "You are joking."

Sherborne tipped his head toward Alastair.

"Mr. Drummond," I said, surprised. "I would not have taken you to be a superstitious man."

"And you would be right. I am not one. But I have seen the weeping woman with my own eyes."

"I've told you before. That was only your reflection in the mirror, Alastair," Gordon said as he passed by his brother, slapping him on the shoulder.

Alastair smiled, but his top lip curled back in frustration, and he kept his eyes on Gordon until he disappeared into his own room. When he turned back to me, his expression was lighter, though I could tell he was still on the defense. "I have never been one to believe in ghosts or spirits or tales of this kind, but I cannot deny my own eyes. I saw the weeping woman standing in a window late one night. I was walking across the grass, and when I looked up, there she was." He pointed to the end of the hallway at the window that looked out in the direction of the stables. "I turned away for a moment, and when I looked back, she was gone."

"Are you certain it was not your mother or a servant?" I asked.

He nodded. "Positive. I had never seen the woman before."

"And he has never seen her since," Sherborne said with a roll of his eyes. "No one has."

Lady Drummond reached out and laid a hand on her son's shoulder. "Alastair does not really believe in the spirit, Alice. He is only trying to scare you on your first evening in the castle."

Alastair's attention turned to his mother sharply, his lips tightening into a thin line, and then he turned back to me with a vacant smile on his face. He did not speak, but I could see the dissenting thoughts running through his mind. If I had to guess, I would have said

Alastair truly believed he'd seen the woman's spirit, but his mother did not want him embarrassing her or himself in front of their guests—especially in front of me, since I was the woman she hoped would one day be his bride.

"I don't know who could be scared in a place like this," my mother said. "The castle truly is lovely. Much cozier than I expected, if I'm being honest."

"We have done our best to make it a welcoming place," Lady Drummond said. "I hope you will both sleep well."

My mother said goodbye to the rest of the party still in the hallway, squeezed my hand, and then went into her own room. Alastair offered to walk me to mine. As we left, Sherborne caught my eye one last time. I thought I noticed something of a head nod or a wink of acknowledgement, but I turned away before I could be sure. I still didn't know I wouldn't tell my mother about the whole ordeal in the morning. Even if Sherborne Sharp left like he promised, I might decide to tell Lady Drummond so she could keep him out of her house and away from her valuables.

Or, I might keep it to myself. I was undecided.

"Your room, my lady," Alastair said, bowing low as though we had been transported back to the time the castle was built. "I look forward to spending the day with you tomorrow."

A line of maids brushed past us carrying extra blankets, delivering them to each room. One girl, pale with red hair and splotches of freckles, handed me a blanket, her hand trembling around the fabric for only a moment, before she dropped it into my hands and hurried to the next room. Alastair did not acknowledge her, his attention trained on me.

I smiled at him and slipped into my room, pressing the door closed silently. Yes, a good night's rest was what I needed to settle my own thoughts. I'd know how to handle everything in the morning.

7

I woke from a dream I couldn't remember, the icy chill of it slipping away as my eyes adjusted to the gloom. The sun was not yet up.

It might have been another nightmare about Edward. Or perhaps Samuel Rigby's tales had left me unsettled. Either way, I sat up in bed and reached down for the spare blanket the maid had left for me. The fire burned low in the fireplace, but I was still shivering. I'd gone to bed in my thickest nightgown and stockings, but it wasn't enough to ease the chill. I couldn't imagine living in Druiminn Castle all the time. Lady Drummond must have grown accustomed to not feeling her fingertips. I pulled the blanket up around my shoulders and rolled to my side, but as I did, I heard a thump in the hallway.

I opened my eyes again, peering straight ahead into the darkness, willing my ears to hear better. I waited for the sound of footsteps—a maid or a guest moving down the hallway towards their room—but nothing came. I had nearly convinced myself it was simply a log shifting in the fireplace when I heard another thud followed by a gurgled scream.

My feet were on the cold floor before I could even think about it. It would have been wise to search for a weapon, like a poker from the fireplace, but I was too surprised to act wisely. Instead, I ran immediately into the hallway with no understanding of what I would find on the other side.

The lamps along the hall had been extinguished when the guests went to bed, so the corridor was dripping in an inky darkness. I stood in my doorway, scanning and listening. Moments later, there was another crash. This time, it was louder and nearer than the first noise. It came from my left, and when I looked in that direction, I saw a clay bowl go rolling across the floor towards me as though someone had knocked over the decorative table on which it had rested.

"Hello?" I called, my voice shaking.

The door across from mine opened, and I flinched before Charles Barry appeared. His blonde hair was sticking in every direction, his eyes half-closed. "What is the disturbance?"

I shook my head. "I don't know. I heard a commotion and came out to—"

Before I could finish the sentence, a figure appeared, stepping forward like a shadow peeling itself from the other shadows.

Charles' eyes widened, and he pulled back into his room until all I could see was the glow of his eyes in the darkness.

"Hello?" I called again, too scared to retreat. "Who are you?""

The figure took a few more stumbling steps forward, and I realized it was a man, hunched forward at the waist. His arms were drawn towards his middle, his head bowed. A rasping wheeze like wind through a loose shutter filled the corridor.

"Are you hurt?" Charles asked from the relative safety of his room.

I wanted to tell him to move into the hall and address the threat so I would not have to, but it was clear that wouldn't happen. So, I took two steps forward. "Please announce yourself. Who are you?"

Suddenly, the man looked up. My eyes had adjusted sufficiently to the darkness that I recognized Alastair Drummond at once. His hair was pasted to his forehead with sweat, his square jaw clenched in a grimace.

"Alastair?" I took another step forward, but then my eyes slid down his tall frame, and I saw the bloom of a dark stain across the front of his shirt, a blade sticking out from the center.

I screamed less out of fear and more out of a need to get other people into the hallway. Alastair was hurt—badly—and I didn't know what to do. Charles Barry had made it clear he wouldn't be of any use, either.

"Mama!" I screamed over my shoulder, backing away from Alastair and towards my mother's room. "Mama!"

Her door opened, and she was at my side in an instant. "What is it, Alice?"

Before I could answer the question, my mother put her arm around my middle and pulled me behind her, placing herself between me and Alastair. She gasped when she saw him. "Alastair?"

The youngest Drummond son fell to his knees, his hands wrapped around the hilt of the blade in his stomach. It looked like he was trying to pull it free from his abdomen, but the hilt was slick with blood, and he couldn't get a grip.

My mother moved towards the young man at once, and I followed behind her. Alastair wobbled forward, and we both caught him before he could fall on his stomach, further burying the blade into his body.

"We need to lay him back," Mama said firmly.

Clumsily and without the help of Charles Barry, who was frozen in his doorway, we laid Alastair on his back just as Gordon Drummond arrived. He shoved my mother aside and knelt next to his brother. Already a puddle of blood was growing beneath Alastair. I could see by the paleness in his face that he was not doing well.

"What happened?" Gordon asked desperately.

I didn't know if he was directing the question at me or Alastair, but it didn't matter. I didn't know and Alastair didn't seem capable of saying. His lips moved around words, but no sound came out except for a ragged wheezing noise.

Gordon got to his feet. "We need to send for a doctor."

"I'll go," Charles said quickly, running from his room and down the hall before Gordon could take a step.

"Tell one of the servants to drive out for the doctor," my mother called after him. "There is no telephone here." Even in the midst of all this, it struck me to be impressed by her presence of mind.

A light at the end of the hall came on. Lady Drummond carried a flickering lamp, not yet aware of what the commotion was, not knowing her son was dying in the middle of the floor. The light was faint and distant, but it did a lot to illuminate the scene.

"He has been stabbed all over," Gordon said, leaning away and shaking his head. He was looking pale, as well.

"Who has been stabbed?" Lady Drummond asked, rushing forward to set her lamp on a small table near the wall. As soon as she saw the scene, her mouth dropped open and her eyes went wide. The only reason she didn't fall on her face was because my mother leaped forward to steady her. "Alastair."

He stirred at the sound of his mother's voice, but he didn't open his eyes.

Gordon laid a hand on his brother's shoulder—one of the only places not covered in blood—and Alastair's mouth began to move again.

"What is he saying?" Lady Drummond asked. Her voice was thick and wobbly. "Who did this?"

Gordon leaned forward, his ear to Alastair's mouth, but I didn't hear the exchange between the brothers because the rest of the party seemed to arrive in the next moment. Vivian Barry came out of her room—the one next to Charles'—and pressed her hand to her lips. Samuel Rigby appeared beside her. They whispered back and forth to one another, shaking their heads and looking bewildered, but they didn't move forward to help. Lord Drummond arrived with his pistol in hand as if expecting a duel. He was the one to call for maids to bring towels and water. Charles Barry came back a few minutes later, assuring Lady Drummond he had sent a servant out to fetch a doctor, but it would be awhile before anyone arrived.

My mother, maintaining a cool air of capability, did her best to put pressure on Alastair's wounds, but it seemed apparent to everyone that there was nothing that could be done.

"What is going on?"

Everyone turned to see Sherborne Sharp walking down the hall. His dark hair was mussed on one side, creases from his pillow on his cheek, but his eyes were wide and alert. He tilted his head to the side, trying to peer around the crowd to the source of the commotion. When he saw Alastair on the floor, he released a choking sound. "What happened?"

"Nobody knows," Vivian Barry answered. "Alice and Charles found him this way."

"Well, he was standing when I saw him," Charles said.

"He has been stabbed," Samuel offered. "That much we know. Otherwise, we aren't sure. Alastair hasn't spoken, and it seems he is unconscious now."

Lady Drummond had dropped to her knees next to Gordon and was running her hand through Alastair's hair, the same red-brown shade as her own. She whispered comforting words to him, but I had a feeling they were more for her than for him.

As far as I could tell, Alastair wasn't aware of much. His breathing was shallow, and his breaths were growing fewer and further between. Despite my mother's efforts to staunch his bleeding, his wounds were too numerous. Blood seemed to pulse from everywhere, the spot on the floor growing to encompass most of the hallway.

By the time the doctor arrived—a gray-haired man in

his nightclothes with a dress coat pulled over the top—Alastair hadn't taken a breath in fifteen minutes. The doctor pronounced him dead on arrival, but it was not news to anyone. We all knew he would die. The only question that needed to be answered now was who was responsible.

8

"It was eerie," Vivian whispered, her hands clutched around a cup of tea. "The way everyone was so quiet. Lady Drummond didn't even scream. They all just...stared at him."

"Screaming wouldn't have helped," her brother said. Charles had his arm around his sister to comfort her, but he looked like he would rather be upstairs in his bed. "It was obvious from the first time I saw him that he would die from his wounds."

"People do not scream to help, Charles. They scream because it is the human instinct. Alice screamed when she saw him."

I felt my cheeks warm. "I wanted to alert everyone to what was going on."

"Don't be embarrassed, Alice," Vivian insisted. "I would have screamed, too. If I'd seen him collapse the way you did, I would have fainted."

We were in the same sitting room we'd been in the night before listening to Samuel Rigby's tales of the castle. Last night it had felt cozy, crowded with people and laughter and firelight. Now, it was cold. No one had bothered to light the fire. It was just my mother, myself, and the Barry siblings on the furniture. Lord and Lady Drummond were talking with the authorities who had arrived with the doctor. Gordon was with them, I presumed, and Samuel Rigby and Sherborne Sharp had made themselves scarce soon after the police arrived.

"I cannot believe we are enduring this again," Charles said. "This is the third time the four of us have been in a house where someone died. If I didn't know any better, I'd think the killer was one of us."

"We don't know that there is a killer," Vivian said sharply.

Charles raised a brow at his sister. "You believe Alastair stabbed himself that many times? There were wounds to his back. How would he have managed those?"

"We should leave those questions for the police to answer," my mother said. "Our duty is to be here for Lord and Lady Drummond during this time. They are beside themselves right now, I'm sure."

Charles nodded, and I saw realization cross his face. My mother would know better than anyone how Lady Drummond was feeling right now. She had seen her own son shot and bleeding before her eyes. And then, she had lost him. No one could understand the pain of losing a child except for a person who had felt it already.

"I want to do something," Mama said, her hands fidgeting in the fabric of her shawl. "Perhaps, I could bring them some tea. Or something to eat."

"I'm sure that's being taken care of. The servants are

at work in the kitchen," I said. "I saw them on my way here. No one can go back to sleep, it seems."

"It isn't even five," Charles lamented. "What was Alastair doing out of bed in the middle of the night?"

My mother shot him a stern look, and Charles bit back his question and any further questions, it seemed. Though, I had similar thoughts.

What had Alastair been doing awake in the middle of the night? Or had he been attacked in his sleep? If so, why had the assailant allowed him to wander the hallways rather than finish the job in his room?

"I would love to be of help, but truthfully, I scarcely know the Drummonds," Vivian admitted. "I met Lady Drummond only twice while she was in London. I enjoyed her company, but I was surprised when she extended an invitation to us."

"I didn't want to come," Charles said.

"But I convinced him," Vivian continued. "A week in Scotland sounded like fun. Of course, now I wish we had stayed home. If I never see another dead body as long as I live, it will still be too soon."

I raised my teacup in agreement.

Charles did the same and then sighed. "After this, I will be perfectly content to never accept another invitation in my life. Staying at home alone is preferable to this."

"I still can't get over it," Vivian said as though her brother hadn't spoken. "The quiet way everyone responded. It was almost as if they were expecting this to happen."

"Don't say that," my mother hissed.

Vivian's eyes went wide. "I'm sorry. I didn't mean—"

"Don't let Lady Drummond or anyone in the family hear you say such a thing," she said. "Of course, they didn't know this would happen. Who would ever think this kind of tragedy would occur?"

"I just meant," Vivian stuttered, her lips trembling. "I just meant that everyone seemed too calm."

"She didn't mean any harm, Mama," I said, laying a hand on my mother's knee. She stilled immediately, her hand coming down to rest on top of mine. She squeezed my fingers, and her hands were ice cold.

"You are frigid." I laid her hand back on her lap and stood up. "Let me find you another blanket and some fresh tea."

She tried to tell me she was fine, but her protests were weak, and I knew my mother well enough to know she was overwhelmed. Her thoughts went to Edward often enough, but a young man of similar age lying dead in a puddle of blood upstairs made it impossible for her not to think even more of my brother. I was struggling with the same issue. Staying busy would help me and hot tea would help her. I set off to find a maid.

The kitchen was accessed by a narrow corridor off of the dining room. The ceilings were lower, making it feel as though the stone ceiling was trying to press down on whoever walked beneath it. I hurried through the space and into the kitchen.

The household staff stood in a small huddle in the middle of the room, whispering so softly their voices were just a faint hiss. The head cook was a burly middle-aged woman with pitch black hair braided down her back and an apron around her waist. She had her arms around a red-haired maid, rubbing her hand along the smaller woman's back. When I cleared my throat, everyone in the room turned to me, including the red-haired maid, who I recognized at once as the young woman who had given me the spare blanket before bed last night. Since she was the only one of the group I recognized, I directed my question to her.

"Could I trouble you for some fresh tea? Ours is going cold."

The maid's green eyes were red and swollen, and she blinked at me for several seconds.

It was the head cook who nodded and answered me. "Yes, someone will bring it right out."

I smiled in sad thanks and left. Even the servants were crying over Alastair. It made sense, of course. A violent death in the house was always distressing. I was just uncomfortable with the fact that I seemed to be the only person in the entire house not devastated by the murder.

It was a tragedy, but I did not know the victim well enough to cry, and each tear I didn't shed felt like an insult to his family. I was a guest in their home. Didn't I owe it to them to be heartbroken? Or was it better to remain stoic and calm? I could be of more help that way, after all.

I sighed, unsure what I was supposed to do or how to help. Perhaps, it would be better if my mother and I left early. We could get a ride to the train station and head for home immediately. Then, my mother would not have to relive Edward's death, and I would not have to fret over how I was supposed to react.

As I stepped out of the servant's corridor and into the dining room, the echo of raised voices reached me. To my knowledge, everyone in the house was either in the sitting room or upstairs, so curiosity compelled me to turn to the right and head in the direction of the library.

The door was partially open, allowing me to see a small sliver of the room. The most I could make out was a black oxford shoe tapping against the floor, but as soon as the conversation picked up again, I didn't need to see any faces to recognize who the voices belonged to.

"What exactly are you suggesting?" Samuel Rigby asked. His voice was soft but defensive. It seemed he had dropped the façade of soothing storyteller that he'd possessed the night before.

The library floor creaked with a footstep and Gordon Drummond moved into view. His face was pale with dark circles under his eyes.

I stepped away from the door before he could see me.

"I'm suggesting you had something to do with my brother's murder," Gordon said.

"Have the police even ruled it a murder?" Samuel asked, echoing Vivian's sentiment from earlier.

Almost as if they had overheard the Barry siblings bickering, Gordon Drummond responded, "I don't need to be a police detective to recognize that my brother couldn't stab himself in his own back."

"And you believe I could have?" Samuel asked.

"Yes, I do," Gordon said. "You told that ridiculous story last night, the tale of the weeping woman. The last words my brother uttered in my ear were, 'the weeping woman in white'. What do you make of that?"

My eyes went wide. I crept forward again, clinging more closely to the doorframe, careful to keep my breathing shallow and silent.

"He was delirious, Gordon. Those who found him

said he stumbled all around the hall. He tripped over a table and sent the contents rolling across the floor," Samuel said. "Clearly, he was not well. Whoever attacked him, assuming he was indeed attacked, did their job thoroughly."

"He was well enough to give me a clue. Well enough to choose those words as his last. I can't believe that doesn't mean anything."

"And I can't allow you to make a mockery of my name and reputation," Samuel said. "I am sorry for your loss, but I've never wished ill upon anyone, your brother included, and you know that."

"I know no such thing." The words were spoken in a half-shout.

I looked around to be sure the sound of their arguing wasn't drawing any other attention. I had received enough ridicule as a girl for eavesdropping that I didn't want to be found with my ear pressed to a door. Especially when the topic of discussion was so serious.

"Think on this for a moment, Gordon. Please. You are not making any sense. If Alastair was capable of whispering a few words in your ear, why not just say my name?" Samuel asked. "Why not make his meaning plain?"

"Had he not been bleeding to death, I suspect he would have made his meaning very plain," Gordon said. "As it was, he did the best he could."

"So, you admit yourself that your brother was confused?"

"There is a difference between being confused and speaking nonsense," Gordon said. "Just because he could not tell me what he wanted to in plain words doesn't mean he didn't tell me the truth."

Samuel sighed. "Why would I come into this house as a guest, only to kill your brother?"

"We both know the answer to that."

"I wish you would enlighten me because I haven't the faintest idea what my supposed motive would be."

"Your daughter." Gordon let the words hang between them. "You blamed Alastair for her death. I heard you accuse him."

Hearing pacing on the other side of the door now, I tucked myself closer to the wall to avoid being seen.

"I was wild with grief when I made that accusation," Samuel answered. "You know I forgave Alastair long ago."

"I know you claimed to," Gordon said. "No one can truly know the contents of a man's heart. It is possible you told Alastair you forgave him all the while harboring ill will towards him. And perhaps, your desire for revenge grew too strong to ignore."

"This is absurd, and I won't—"

"May I search your room?" Gordon asked, interrupting Samuel's defense. "Would I find a woman's white gown there? It would be a fitting revenge, wouldn't it? Killing Alastair dressed as a scorned lover?"

"Jenny was never his lover," Samuel bit back. "And you would do well not to mention her again. You are lashing out in grief just as I did all those years ago. I am trying to overlook your cruelty, but push, and you may find my forgiveness has a limit."

My attention was fully trained on the crack in the library door. My heart was pounding, and I couldn't move. Had Samuel Rigby killed Alastair? It hardly seemed possible, but then, I knew very little about the man. I hadn't known he'd had a daughter. Especially not a daughter who would have been old enough to be in a romantic relationship with Alastair Drummond.

I heard Gordon unhitch his breath to respond, but before he could, there were footsteps behind me.

"Miss Beckingham? I was just bringing your tea."

I startled at the unexpected voice and spun around, my hip knocking into the corner of a small shelf. I quickly steadied a picture frame before it could tip over. When I looked up, it was to see an unfamiliar maid, a blonde woman not much older than me, calmly holding a tray of tea.

She seemed oblivious to how badly she had fright-ened me. "Shall I leave the tea here or take it to the sitting room?" she asked.

I moved away from the door, doing my best to keep my expression calm while hoping beyond hope that the men in the library had not heard the maid. "The sitting room will do. Thank you."

The maid nodded, but before she could leave, her eyes shifted to look over my shoulder.

I felt a draft against my back and knew the library door was fully open now. I turned to see Gordon Drum-mond standing in the doorway. His red hair was disheveled and sticking in every direction as though his fingers had been run through it nervously, but his eyes were clear and focused. I felt my skin heat as he stared at me, all possibility that he didn't know I'd been eavesdrop-ping on his conversation slipping away. He knew.

Samuel Rigby appeared over Gordon's shoulder, and when he saw me, he dropped his gaze, as if embarrassed.

I expected a confrontation but before anyone could say anything, the maid spoke up again. "Oh, Miss Beckingham?"

I turned to her slowly, not wanting my back to be against Gordon. He had given me that bit of advice the day before. At the time, he'd been discussing animals, but he'd made it clear it referred to people, too. Interesting, then, that his brother was stabbed in the back that very night. Clearly, Gordon had never shared that advice with Alastair.

"Yes?" I answered the maid.

"I almost forgot to tell you. The police are beginning their interviews, and they wished to speak with you first. Since you found—" She glanced back at Gordon and bit her lip. "Since you were the first person to find..." Clearly, she did not know how to finish the sentence without referring to Alastair as "the body".

I rescued her by nodding in thanks, and she left quickly, obviously relieved to be free of the tension.

I took a deep breath, turned to face Gordon, and gave a small nod. "If you'll excuse me."

He didn't move or acknowledge me in any way other than tracking my movement with his eyes. I felt his attention on me until I turned into the entrance hall, where I found two policemen waiting for me.

9

The policemen wore dark pants and coats, their silver buttons shining in the light from the lamps, their hats resting in their laps. They leaned forward as they questioned me.

"You came out of your room when you heard the victim scream?" Sergeant Finley asked. He was a round man with a soft face and kind eyes. The opposite of his partner.

"He did not scream," Detective Cavins said with a frustrated sigh. "Miss Beckingham screamed when she saw his wounds."

I nodded and smiled warmly at Sergeant Finley. "Detective Cavins is correct. I came out of my room when I heard a banging sound from the hall. I believe that was Alastair stumbling over things in the corridor but it was too dark to tell for certain."

"So, you did not see anyone else in the hall?" Detective Cavins asked.

"No, I did not. I could scarcely see across the corridor, let alone down the length of it."

Sergeant Finley jotted down my answers in his notebook. I wanted to read what he was writing. I hadn't done anything wrong, of course, but being interviewed still set me on edge.

"Do you know anyone who might have been angry with Mr. Drummond? Had he argued with anyone recently or talked with you about anyone who might have threatened him?"

Gordon and Samuel's conversation in the library came to mind. If Gordon was right and Alastair had caused the death of Samuel's daughter, then Samuel had a good reason to be angry. Still, I had no proof to back up this possibility other than one heated conversation I was not meant to overhear anyway. It felt wrong to throw suspicion on a man when I wasn't even sure the accuser would feel the same way in a day's time. If Gordon wanted the police to look into Samuel as a possible murderer, he would tell them what he knew.

"I'm sorry, gentlemen, but I only met the Drummond family yesterday," I said with a shrug. "My mother knows Lady Drummond, but even they have only met a handful of times. It is a sad coincidence that we were here to witness Alastair's death. If I knew more, I would tell you, but I'm afraid there isn't anything more I can say to help."

Detective Cavins pressed his lips together until they turned white while Sergeant Finley escorted me out.

"Thank you for your assistance, Miss Beckingham," he said, opening the study door. As soon as I stepped into the hall, the door closed, and I was alone.

It did not last long, however. When I reached the top

of the stairs, I saw Sherborne Sharp ascending them. His head was down, so he did not see me until he was halfway up. When he did finally look up, he paused for a moment, and then sighed and finished his ascent.

"I suspect you told the police about my criminal ways?"

"There were more important matters to discuss than petty theft," I said. Though, in truth, I'd forgotten about finding Sherborne in my mother's room the night before. With everything that had happened afterwards, it had slipped my mind. Now, I wondered whether I shouldn't have mentioned it.

His dark brows rose in genuine surprise. "So, you didn't mention the way you found me last night?"

I shook my head. "No."

His shoulders sagged in relief. "Thank you."

"Should I have told them?" Sherborne and I, though newly acquainted, were far beyond the need for discretion in our conversations.

Sherborne reached down to adjust the sleeve of his jacket. The rest of the house was in disarray, but he was sharply dressed, wearing a dark suit with a crisp white shirt underneath. He looked ready to attend church. "I can understand your unease. When one is embroiled in one criminal activity, it is not so odd to think that he could also be embroiled in another."

It was my turn to look surprised. I'd expected him to immediately defend himself, yet, he was laying out an argument against his innocence.

"You have only seen one side of my character, Alice, and that is my fault," he said, folding his hands behind his back. "I gave you a glimpse of the darkest part of me, and I regret you saw that. However, I have to make it clear that what you glimpsed last night was, indeed, the darkest part of me. Thievery is as far as my criminal activity has ever gone."

"Thieves are liars," I reminded him.

"True." He nodded. "And yet, while murderers are likely to be thieves, thieves are not often murderers."

"Do you mean to confuse me, Mr. Sharp?" I understood his meaning well enough, but I did not need him to explain probability to me. Rather, I needed him to explain his own actions to me.

"I mean to tell you that I am not a murderer," he said. "And certainly not the killer of one of my oldest friends. Not only would it be unthinkable to harm Alastair, but what gain would it bring me? If I am nothing more than a thief, as you believe me to be, what would I gain by murdering one of my wealthiest friends?"

Disgust must have been written plainly on my face because Sherborne held up his hands in defense. "I am only making that argument to match your low opinion of me. I would never hurt Alastair because I liked him, but as you seem to think me a man incapable of emotional attachment, I thought I would introduce a more practical defense."

My opinion of Sherborne was not quite as low as he seemed to think it was, but I saw no reason to inform him of that. His fear that I would tell his secret was a weapon in my hands, and I did not want to relinquish it too quickly.

"You seem to have given this a lot of thought," I said. "Innocent men do not spend nearly so much time formulating a defense."

"Being prepared is not a crime," he said. Then, he stepped forward and lowered his voice further. I wanted to step away from him and put more space between us, but I did not want to give him the illusion that I was afraid of him. So, I stood firm. "Speaking of my defense, I'm afraid I will not be able to leave this morning as I promised you I would," he said.

He glanced at the study door, ensuring it was still closed. "I truly did plan to leave, but with Alastair's death, it would look suspicious if I departed too quickly, especially when I originally planned to stay for the week. I don't want to give the police any reason to look into my background."

"Your background should be clean. That is what you told me last night, after all. Stealing my mother's jewelry was your first attempt at thievery, was it not?"

His jaw clenched and then a smile pulled up the right side of his mouth. "You cannot expect me to expose all of my secrets to you, Miss Alice. You have one thing to hold over my head already. I will not supply you with another."

"Besides," he continued. "I do not want to leave. Alastair was good to me. I want to be here to support his family and help uncover what exactly happened to him."

"What do you think happened to him?" I asked, remembering the questions the police had asked me. I knew nothing of the details of Alastair's life, but Sherborne would know. He would know if Alastair was in trouble or if he'd angered anyone. He could be a key player in solving the crime.

Sherborne shook his head. "I wish I knew."

The study door opened with a loud squeal of its

hinges, and Sherborne leaned around me to smile at Detective Cavins, who was scowling. "Sorry, Detective. I hope I haven't kept you waiting long."

Detective Cavins looked at me, his top lip pulling back, and then shook his head. "Not long. But do hurry. We have many more interviews to conduct."

Before I could resist, Sherborne grabbed my hand in an exaggerated gesture, brought my knuckles to his lips, and walked around me and into the study. The door closed with a soft click, and I was once again alone in the hallway, wondering if that kiss to my hand had been a plea for my continued silence.

I wanted desperately to stand outside the study door and listen in on Sherborne's interview, but I could not risk being caught by the police. Though I had nothing to do with Alastair's murder, I did not need to give the authorities any reason to suspect me. I had been in the proximity of several different murders in the past, and although the guilty parties had all been caught, it was still an uncanny coincidence. Anyway, my own brother had been convicted of murder. What if the police believed murderous tendencies ran in the family?

Thoughts of Edward and murder led me understandably to thoughts of my brother's death two years ago. We knew how he died—stabbed during a prison fight—but the person responsible for his death was never named. The authorities told us it was an unfortunate accident. A fight that got out of control. But we had always longed for a more definitive answer than that. And it was that desire for answers that now made me want to help the Drummonds in any way I could. I didn't know much about their family or Alastair's life, but I could learn. I could ask questions just as well as any police detective. Even better, perhaps, since the family and their guests would not be as on edge around me.

A few years ago, I never would have considered such a thing, but since then, I had seen Rose get to the bottom of several crimes. Though my "cousin" was not really my family by blood, I had learned much from watching her. Why shouldn't I apply the courage and careful reasoning Rose had taught me to solving the puzzle of Alastair's murder?

I decided then and there that I would do exactly that. I would brave all dangers in pursuit of the killer.

10

One by one, the guests in Druiminn Castle were called to the study to talk with the police, and one by one, they returned to the party claiming they had no information to share.

Everyone waited in the sitting room, the fire roaring to combat the overcast, gloomy day outside. Any conversations that were had were whispered and infrequent. No one knew what to say, and with our hosts secluding themselves in their bedrooms, devastated with grief, it seemed best to say little at all.

Finally, Vivian Barry returned to the sitting room after her interview, her eyes ringed in red, a handkerchief held to her nose.

"The police are leaving now," she said, taking the seat next to her brother. He laid his arm over her shoulders. "I was the last person they needed to speak with."

"What did you tell them?" Samuel Rigby asked. He had been in the sitting room for over an hour and had not looked at me once. He probably thought I'd told the police what I'd overheard in the library. Or, at the very least, that I had shared the conversation with someone else.

"The truth," Vivian said. "That I don't know anything. That I hardly know the family at all."

Someone cleared their throat, and we all turned to see the policemen, Detective Cavins and Sergeant Finley, in the doorway.

"Thank you all for your cooperation," Sergeant Finley said. "We are sorry for your loss and extend our deepest sympathies."

"Lord and Lady Drummond wished for us to relay what information we can to their guests," Detective Cavins added. "The information we can share is this. We believe Alastair Drummond was stabbed in his bedroom, after which he stumbled out into the hall, where he died. A window in the bedroom was open, leading us to believe the killer gained entry to the castle through that means and then escaped in the same way."

"You believe the murder was random?" Charles Barry asked.

"It seems likely," Sergeant Finley said. "We suspect that the window was used to gain access to the bedroom, where an item of value was stolen. Whether or not the killer knew the victim remains to be seen."

"An item of value?" Sherborne asked, brows pinched together. Of course that was what would interest him most. He was nothing if not predictable.

"Lady Drummond noticed the item missing from her son's room, but we will not be announcing what it was just yet," answered Sergeant Finley.

"Because there's a chance the killer could be someone

inside the castle?" Vivian asked, glancing around nervously. "Or in this very room?"

"All possibilities must be looked into," Detective Cavins said, seeming deliberately vague. "Using the interviews we conducted and our own investigation, we hope to bring the killer to justice as soon as possible."

"And what are we to do until then?" Samuel Rigby asked, standing up. His hands were fists at his side. "Are we permitted to leave?"

Sergeant Finley tilted his head to the side, his mouth twisted into a grave expression. "No, I'm afraid we will have to ask you all to remain here for a few days longer."

"A few days?" Charles looked at his sister, eyes wide. "You really expect us to live at the site of a murder?"

"The victim's remains have been removed from the scene," Sergeant Finley said, as if that should make us feel better. "The coroner came only a while ago, so the young man's body will be examined soon, which we hope will answer even more of our questions. We are optimistic that this case will be resolved shortly."

"And what if it is not?" Charles asked. "Are we to live here forever?"

"Of course not, sir," Sergeant Finley started, sounding frustrated for the first time since I had met him.

"You are to remain here until we say otherwise." Detective Cavins stepped forward, towering over Charles Barry until the young man lowered his head and sat down sheepishly. "Thank you all for your cooperation. We will see you soon," Cavins added with finality.

When the front doors closed behind the officers, the house exploded into chaos. Not only had a man been murdered, but now none of the guests were permitted to leave.

Even if the police changed their minds and decided we could all go home soon, it seemed to me that crucial evidence might well be taken away from the scene. So, if this case was going to be resolved at all, it would have to happen in the next day or two. It had to be soon, which meant it had to be me.

Soon after the police left, my mother pulled me aside near the fireplace, the crackling of the wood drowning out our voices to ensure we had privacy.

"Alice, please promise me you will be careful for the rest of our stay," she said, her cold fingers wrapped tightly around my wrist.

"Mama, of course I will be," I said. "No one here is after me."

"You do not know that," she said. "We can't guess who did this or what their motive was. I think you should sleep in my room tonight."

"Let's not panic unnecessarily," I suggested.

"I am not panicked," she snapped back. "I am looking out for my daughter. You are in this castle because of me, and I will not allow you to be harmed."

I laid my other hand over my mother's, prying her fingers from my wrist, and massaged her cold fingers with my own. "Even if something did happen to me, it would not be your fault. You are not responsible for any of this. Anyway, I'm sure the police will get to the bottom of everything soon."

That was not exactly the truth. I had seen enough of police investigations over the last several years to have my doubts about their methods and accuracy, but I did not want to worry my mother. Mostly because if she was fastened to my side, I would not be able to do any investigating. She would never allow it.

"I hope you are right," she said, turning to look down at the fire. "I cannot believe our week away has turned into this."

Before I could attempt to comfort her, the room around us grew suddenly hushed, and I turned to see Lord and Lady Drummond stepping into the room, Gordon trailing behind them. Despite the tough demeanor Gordon had worn yesterday, he looked every part the dutiful son standing over his mother's shoulder.

"Hello," Lady Drummond said, her voice immediately breaking around the word. She dabbed at her nose with a tissue and cleared her throat. "We are...obviously devastated by what has happened. And we...we—"

Her lips trembled and Lord Drummond stepped forward, a hand laid on his wife's shoulder. For the first time since I'd met him, he was understandably not wearing his signature smile. "We are sorry that you all have been pulled into this," he said. "The police have alerted us to their decision that everyone should remain on the premises. In order to make this difficult time pass more swiftly for all, we want you to spend your next few days here following the activities previously arranged. As much as possible, please try and stick to a normal routine and enjoy yourselves."

Gordon winced and looked off to his right, his eyes trained on the floor. I had a similar feeling. How was anyone meant to enjoy themselves after such a tragedy, especially when they could be in the company of a murderer? It was understandable that the Drummonds didn't want us moping about underfoot, and maybe it would even be helpful for all of our nerves to have some distraction, but how could we possibly pretend everything was normal?

Lord Drummond continued, "The stables are still open and our estate manager, Mr. Kentworth, has kindly volunteered to lead the hunt tomorrow, should some of the gentlemen still wish to go." He wrung his hands in front of him and glanced down at his wife. It was clear she was usually the one to address their guests and make these kinds of announcements. "I suppose that is all for now. Again, we are sorry."

Lady Drummond sniffled and hunched forward, as if weakened with sorrow, and her husband pulled her into a comforting embrace. All of the guests remained frozen, unsure what to do or say that could soothe the woman, but only my mother moved forward. As she crossed the room, everyone turned away, relieved they didn't have to do anything.

I couldn't hear what my mother said, but whatever it was caused Lady Drummond to turn away from her husband and embrace my mother. Still holding on, the two women walked out of the room together, Lord Drummond following behind. Only Gordon remained in the doorway. His arms were crossed, his shoulder leaning against the frame. And though I never caught him directly, I could feel him watching me as I moved around the room.

"It looks as though I didn't have much of a choice in whether I remained here or not," Sherborne said, walking around me to stand where my mother had been just minutes ago.

"It appears not," I said. "I must admit I'm a little glad for it."

He wrinkled his forehead. "I can't understand why anyone would be glad to be locked in an ancient castle after a man has been murdered."

I shook my head. "I'm glad you remained here."

Sherborne raised an eyebrow, a smirk playing on his mouth. "Now, I am even more perplexed. I thought you despised me."

"That remains to be seen," I said. "I do think you could be useful, however."

Any sign of amusement was gone. "How so?"

"Clearly you are skilled at sneaking around."

"Clearly not," he argued. "You found me out."

I ignored this. "In exchange for keeping your secret, I want you to help me find Alastair's murderer."

"So you no longer think I could be guilty of the crime?" he asked quietly.

"I hope this decision will not prove to be a foolish one, but no, I do not think you killed Alastair Drummond." That was not entirely true, but at the moment, Sherborne Sharp was the only person I could think of to ask for help. If he was the killer, it was better that he think I trusted him to keep me from being his next victim. If he was not the killer, then his skills could be useful in tracking down the person or persons responsible.

"What do you want me to do?" he asked.

I glanced towards where Gordon was standing in the doorway. Once again, I didn't see him looking at me, but it seemed as though his eyes had darted away from me just a second before mine landed on him. "I want you to talk to Gordon," I said. "You are closer with the Drummond family than I am, and I want to know who Gordon most suspects."

I'd overheard Gordon's conversation with Samuel Rigby, but I didn't want to move forward based on one emotional outburst. If Gordon felt compelled to mention his theory to someone a second time, then it would mean he truly believed it a possibility.

Sherborne shook his head.

"Would you rather I told everyone what you were doing in my mother's room last night?" I threatened.

He pulled away from me, surprise flicking across his face. "Remind me to never forget how ruthless you can be, Alice Beckingham. I'm only refusing because Gordon will not tell me anything."

"Why not?"

"He has never liked me," Sherborne said with a shrug. "I have been friends with Alastair for years, but Gordon never found a reason to talk to me that didn't include insulting me or suggesting it would be best if I left and never returned. Especially now that he is emotional, I am the last person he will want to talk to. You would have much better luck."

"Me?" I asked, shoulders sagging. "He hardly knows me."

"Which I think may work in your favor," he said. "Plus, you are a beautiful woman. Gordon would never admit it, but much like his brother, he has a soft spot for beauty. He may be surly, but I suspect you would be able to get some information out of him."

I wanted to argue, but it seemed pointless. I didn't have anyone else I could trust, and if Sherborne couldn't get the answers, then I would have to. I sighed. "Fine. I will speak with Gordon, but I would like for you to try and figure out what is missing from Alastair's room. The police wouldn't say, but I'm sure the Drummonds know what it is."

"Ask Gordon," he said.

"I will, obviously, but he may not answer me. And even if he does, it would be good to hear it from two different sources. Easier to verify that way."

Sherborne clicked his heels together and lifted a flat hand to his brow, saluting me. "Aye."

"Put your hand down," I hissed, glancing around to be sure no one saw.

Sherborne lowered his hand and shrugged. "I have my orders. Go do what you need to do."

Feeling less and less confident with every second, I walked away from Sherborne Sharp, praying he was not as incompetent as he appeared.

Gordon didn't look at me as I walked towards him, but I could tell by the shift in his posture that he knew I was coming.

"I'm sorry for your loss," I said.

He tilted his head almost imperceptibly, looking at me out of the corner of his eye. "Thank you."

"I know we discussed my feelings about Alastair yesterday, but I hope you know those were purely about any romantic involvement with him." I could feel my cheeks flushing, embarrassed at having to discuss this at all. "Beyond what little time I spent with him, I didn't know him well enough to make any judgment of him, though he seemed very kind."

Gordon nodded, his chin jutting out, and then he

turned to face me, pressing his back against the door-frame. "Are you attempting to inform me you did not have cause to murder my brother?"

My mouth hung open for a moment, as I was too star-tled to come up with a response. When I did, it was stam-mered and nervous. "That was not—My intention in coming over here was to...to offer my condolences."

"Which you have done," Gordon said, giving me a tight, dismissive smile.

I shifted my feet and folded my hands behind my back, trying not to look half as uncomfortable as I felt. "I wondered if you wouldn't be looking for someone to talk with. I'm sure this has all been very overwhelming for you and your family, and I just wanted to offer you my ear should you need it."

"Is that what you were doing this morning?" Gordon pushed away from the doorframe and stood tall, towering over me. I had to tilt my head back to meet his eyes. "Were you lurking outside of the library and listening to a private conversation because you thought I might be in need of companionship?"

Heat rolled down my neck and back as shame gripped me. Still, I lifted my chin and met his accusation head on. "Accidentally overhearing a loud conversation as I passed by a room can hardly be called eavesdropping."

"Were you passing by?" he asked. "It seemed to me you were rather stationary."

There was no sense in denying the obvious. Clearly, Gordon knew I'd been listening in on his conversation, and if I had any chance of him being honest with me, then I would have to be honest with him and admit that.

"And it seemed to me," I said, taking a step toward him, voice low, "that you were involved in a very heated debate only hours after the murder of your brother. Excuse me for being worried about your safety."

In actuality, Gordon's safety was not my primary motivator, but it wasn't vital that he know that.

He raised his right eyebrow, suspicious, and I looked away towards the rest of the guests in the sitting room. No one seemed to be paying us any attention. Everyone was so concerned with themselves and how this was affecting them that they couldn't see beyond that. Perhaps, that distraction could be used to my benefit over the next several days.

"Do you truly expect me to believe my safety was your main concern?" he asked. "Before yesterday, we did not even know one another. What could I have done in such a short amount of time to earn such high regard?"

"You sounded adamant that you had caught your brother's murderer, and if so, I did not want you to find the same fate. That seems like common decency to me."

"Do you expect me to thank you?" he asked.

"Do you expect me to apologize?" I challenged. "Because I will not. I did nothing wrong. According to you, it is Samuel Rigby who has done something. Have you told the police of your suspicions? It is unsafe to let the man roam free if you believe—"

"My suspicions are my own business," Gordon interrupted, clenching his jaw. "And again, I do not believe your eavesdropping had anything to do with my safety or anyone else's."

"You think so little of yourself?" I asked. "You don't

think it could be possible that anyone would be worried about you?"

"It is possible," he said. "But given the other evidence, I doubt concern for me was the driving force that led you to stand outside the library door."

"Evidence?" I asked, forehead wrinkled. "What are you referring to?"

He folded his arms over his chest and shrugged. "I'm simply referring to the facts: you did not want to be at the castle this weekend, you made it known you had no interest in Alastair, and you were the first person out of the entire house to find his body. All of that, paired with the fact that I found you lurking outside of a room listening to my conversation, points to the possibility that you could somehow be involved."

"Involved in your brother's murder?" I asked, eyes wide. "Tell me you aren't serious."

"Tell me you were truly eavesdropping on my conversation out of concern for me," he challenged.

"On what grounds do you suggest otherwise?" I snapped.

"How firmly was your mother trying to force you and my brother together?" he asked. "A desire to make your own love match could be more than enough reason to—"

"To murder someone?" I shook my head in disgust. "If you think that is cause for murder then perhaps the police should look more closely at you."

His eyes flared with anger, and I wanted to apologize as soon as the words were out of my mouth, but I couldn't. My pride wouldn't allow it. Instead, I clenched my fists and narrowed my eyes.

"I charged you with underestimating people's affection for you and concern for your wellbeing, but perhaps I was the one who made an incorrect estimation. With every opportunity I have to know you better, I find myself less interested in the man I find."

"Be that as it may," Gordon said, leaning back against the doorframe and looking into the sitting room. "My accusation stands."

"As does mine," I said before turning on my heel and taking the stairs to the next floor two at a time, leaving Gordon behind.

11

J ust as I reached the top of the stairs, my mother came out of Lady Drummond's room. Her face was red and splotched, her eyes swollen. When she saw me, she dabbed at her eyes and smiled.

"Oh, Alice. You didn't need to come check on me."

I decided not to tell her that hadn't been my intention at all. "How are the Drummonds doing?"

"As well as can be expected," she said. "I actually only came out to send for some tea. They haven't had anything to eat or drink all morning."

"You stay," I said, turning back towards the stairs. "I'll go down to the kitchen."

"I would be happy to go to the kitchen for you," said an unexpected voice.

I turned to see a red-haired maid standing in the middle of the hallway, her arms full of white sheets. "I just need to drop this in with the laundry first."

Her voice was thick and raw, and I recognized her as the young maid from the kitchens, the one who had been so distraught. I tried to remember her name and thought I had heard her called Hester at some point.

"That would be wonderful," my mother said.

"And maybe bring up something small to eat," I said as the maid passed. "Some toast, perhaps."

She looked up and nodded, her green eyes red-rimmed. "Of course, Miss Beckingham."

"Thank you, Hester."

When I said her name, she stiffened slightly, but then carried on down the stairs.

"Well, I suppose—" I started, taking a step towards my room.

"I'm sure Lord and Lady Drummond would like to see you," Mama said.

"Oh, I'm not sure I'd be of much help," I said. Though, I had just offered the same services to Gordon downstairs.

My mother moved towards me, head low. "Surely you remember what it felt like to be in their situation, Alice. They are in need of distraction. Anything to pull their attention away from their loss for even a moment."

Unable to argue, I nodded and followed my mother into the room.

The space was dark. No one had pulled the curtains open yet. Lady Drummond, wearing her dressing gown, was sitting in bed beneath the blankets, while her husband paced the room distractedly.

"Eleanor?" Lady Drummond asked, turning towards the door.

"I sent for tea," my mother said, crossing the room and taking her friend's hand. "And Alice is here with me."

Alastair's mother closed her eyes and shook her head. "You two are so kind to us. I'm so glad to have met you."

"And I you," my mother said.

"I know Alastair would have grown to be very fond of you, too, Alice," Lady Drummond said, turning her attention to me.

The woman sitting before me looked twenty years older than the woman I'd met the day before. Her face was lined and creased, and her eyes drooped as though they were trying to drip down her face. Grief had taken a toll on her.

"He was a very kind young man," I said, wondering how many times I would be forced to pretend I knew anything about Alastair from the five minutes we'd spent together since my arrival.

"He was," Lady Ashton said, choking on a sob. "He was a good son, too. A very obedient boy, even as a small child. We only had to discipline him once before he would learn his lesson and mind. Even when he went off to school."

"We thought he might have been too young to go away to school," Lord Drummond said, finally pausing in his pacing to join in on the conversation.

He offered a small smile, but there was a wistfulness to it that let me know he was not happy in any real sense of the word. His eyes were foggy and distant, as if he was remembering a long ago memory. Which, I supposed, he was.

"Yes, we were hesitant to send him," Lady Drummond said. "But in the end, Alastair convinced us."

"As he often did," Lord Drummond chuckled, pressing a knuckle to his lips.

"He was ready to advance in his studies, so we allowed him to go." Lady Drummond grabbed my mother's hand and set it in her lap, clinging to it the way a child might cling to a blanket. "And you know? He wrote us every week. He sent letters, updating us on the young friends he was making and his experience. Even far away, he tried to stay near."

"It sounds like you were all very close," my mother said.

"Extremely," Lord Drummond said heavily.

Just then, the red-haired maid knocked on the door and came in with a tray of tea. She looked at the Drummonds only once before quickly ducking her head and going about her work.

I could not blame here. I didn't much want to share the space with them, either.

"Thank you, Hester," Lady Drummond said. As soon as the maid left the room, the door closing behind her, Lady Drummond pressed her lips together and shook her head. "Alastair was truly beloved. Even the servants are heartbroken at his loss."

"Yes, the poor girl did look distressed," my mother said. "She is clearly mourning him."

"Well, I am not surprised," Lord Drummond said. "Alastair had a keen eye for two things: pheasant shooting and pretty girls."

Lady Drummond laughed sadly and nodded her head to me. "That is proven by Alice being here. Alastair was saying just last night what a lovely girl you are, dear."

My face warmed at the attention, and I nodded, doing my best to look grateful.

My mother stood up and fetched the tray from the

table in the corner, carrying it to the side of the bed. "Won't you two try and eat something? There's fresh tea, as well as some toast."

"I couldn't," Lady Drummond said, laying a hand on her stomach and waving away the tray with the other. "I can't imagine eating anything at all right now."

"It seems futile," Lord Drummond said blankly, his eyes cold and staring at the wall ahead.

"Don't say that," my mother said, brows pulled together in sympathy. "I know it seems daunting now, but you cannot give up."

Lady Drummond looked stricken for a moment, but then all at once, her face crumpled, and she was sobbing. Lord Drummond didn't even rush over to comfort her.

"How are we supposed to carry on?" Lady Drummond asked. Then, she sat up and grabbed my mother's hands. "How did you do it, Eleanor? When Edward passed away, how did you cope?"

I folded my hands behind my back and then brought them around to the front, unsure whether I was supposed to stay for this part of the conversation or not.

"There aren't any rules for this kind of pain," my mother said, her voice growing thick with every word.

I moved towards the door slowly, hoping not to attract too much attention.

"The most important thing is to rely on one another," she said, looking between the two Drummonds. "And on your family."

"Gordon," Lady Drummond gasped. "I have been so distracted, I haven't even looked in on him. He will be just as distressed as we are."

"I will send for him," Lord Drummond assured her.

My mother started to stand up, but I quickly jumped in. "I will find Gordon and send him up."

Lady Ashton's face softened, her lower lip jutting out. "Thank you, Alice."

I smiled and slipped from the room gratefully.

NOT WANTING to talk to Gordon again so soon after he pointed the finger at me for murdering his brother, I went down and asked one of the servants outside the kitchen to deliver the message to him that he was needed in his parents' room. Then, I walked through the library and onto the terrace, taking a deep breath of the fresh air.

It hadn't even been a day since Alastair's death and already I was feeling stifled. I couldn't imagine how I would feel after several more days trapped in the castle.

Hopefully the killer would be brought to justice quickly and it wouldn't come to that.

I tipped my head back and looked up at the sky. It was gloomy, the clouds heavy and gray, but the breeze was crisp. I folded my arms around my midsection, shivering.

I'd only been back to my room for a few minutes since Alastair's death. Just long enough to change into a simple dark blue skirt with a cream blouse. I'd been in such a rush to get away from the crime scene that I'd left my shawl in my room, and now I was wishing for it.

I had half a mind to turn around and go fetch it, even knowing there was a risk I would be stopped by my mother and pulled into the Drummonds' bedroom again, but then I saw Samuel Rigby sitting out on the lawn.

Ignoring the scattered lawn furniture, he had his

brown suit jacket spread out on the grass beneath him and was sitting on it with a book balanced on his knees. He didn't appear to have noticed my presence and seemed very deep in thought. I didn't know when the opportunity to speak to him alone would arise again. With all of the guests stuck in the house together, finding alone time was not likely to be easy.

As I got closer, I could see that Mr. Rigby was not reading a book but writing in a journal. His head was bent low, eyebrows furrowed and pulled together as his hand flew across the page. He was writing so quickly I almost felt guilty when the sound of my footsteps broke his concentration.

He looked up, startled, and then his eyes focused on me.

"Miss Alice."

He did not look either pleased or displeased to see me, which I considered a good sign.

"Mr. Rigby." I tipped my head slightly and then waved a hand towards the spot in the grass next to him. "Do you mind if I join you?"

I could tell immediately he wanted to say no. Clearly, he had come outside to escape the rest of the guests in the castle. Still, he was too polite to say so and reluctantly invited me to sit. So, I did.

"This trip has proven to be much more eventful than I planned for."

"Yes, indeed." He nodded. "A terrible turn of events."

We sat quietly together, neither of us sure how to carry the conversation forward. So, I opted for directness.

"I hope you can forgive me for overhearing your conversation this morning with Mr. Drummond."

Samuel lifted his eyebrows and nodded. "The door was open, so it wasn't as though we took great measures to keep it private."

Again, he was far too polite to point out, the way Gordon had, that I was eavesdropping rather than simply overhearing something.

"I was still fumbling through things after the excitement of the morning," I said. "If I'd had my wits about me, I like to think I would have turned away once the conversation veered into personal matters. But as it was, I intruded upon your privacy and for that, I'm sorry."

Mr. Rigby smiled. "Forgiven, Miss Alice. Of course."

I smiled in return and tucked my legs to the side, folding my hands in my lap. "Though, Mr. Rigby, since I did overhear a bit of the conversation, I wondered if I could ask you a question?"

He tensed immediately and closed the journal he'd been writing in, tucking it against his leg. "I was actually thinking about heading back up to the house soon. It's becoming a little too cool outdoors for me."

"Oh, of course. This will only take a second," I assured him.

He pulled on his jacket, adjusting the collar around his neck and nodded with a quick sigh. "All right. Yes, you may ask."

"Since you have forgiven me for listening in," I said, reminding him of his forgiveness in the hope he would not repeal it once I asked my question, "I suppose I will be frank. I overheard mention of your daughter?"

Samuel glanced down at the grass and then seemed to follow the slope of the hill down and back up to the horizon. "Yes," he breathed. "I had a daughter."

"And you don't still?"

"No," he said, turning to me with a polite smile. "I don't."

"How did she die?" I asked quietly.

Mr. Rigby breathed in as though he was about to speak, but then nothing came out. We just sat in silence that stretched on for seconds, growing more uncomfortable with every moment. Then, he shook his head. "You overheard that my daughter was dead and that I blamed Alastair for it, correct?"

I turned to look at him. His face was red, eyes downcast. "I did."

He sighed. "Well, let me make it clear right now that I do not believe Alastair had anything to do with my daughter's death."

"All right, but why would you have blamed him in the first place?"

"Miss Alice," he warned. I recognized the tone in his voice. It was the same way my father would say my name when I became too passionate at the dinner table or asked too many questions of our guests. It was meant to calm me down, but instead only made me more determined to do or say whatever I'd been planning to.

"I am not trying to pry, Mr. Rigby," I added quickly. "I hope I am not making you uncomfortable."

"Well," he said. "It is not a very pleasant topic to discuss."

"I'm sure it isn't." A particularly cool breeze moved through, making me clutch my skirt around my legs and Mr. Rigby shiver slightly. I had to act quickly if I wanted to get any information from him. I shifted my body towards him, head and voice low. "I would never want to abuse the information I overheard this morning, but the fact of the matter is that I heard a compelling argument for why it is you could have been angry with Alastair, and I only wonder—"

"Did you say anything to the police?" he asked suddenly, eyes narrowed.

"No," I said truthfully. "I wanted to give you the opportunity to explain the other side of the situation before I said anything."

He leaned away from me, his mouth a hard, flat line. "So, you do intend to share what you heard?"

I opened my mouth to explain, to try and gather up the broken fragments of this conversation and piece them back together, but before I could, Samuel stood up, brushed off his trousers, and looked down at me.

"Forgive me, Miss Beckingham, but I believe you have heard as much on this particular subject as you are going to from me," he said sharply. "I realize we do not know one another well and what you think of me, I have no idea, but for what it matters, I would prefer if you did not mention what you heard to anyone else."

"I think highly of you, Mr. Rigby," I said desperately. "I hope I did not imply otherwise."

"Regardless," he said, holding up a hand to quiet me. "The matter you overheard was a sensitive subject to both families. Mr. Drummond has only just lost his brother and anything he said surely came from a place of grief and distress and should not be taken seriously. Just as what I said to Gordon all those years ago was nothing more than a wild accusation born from a weak mind and heart."

I stood up, moving towards Mr. Rigby, but he backed

away from me quickly and shook his head. "I'm sure you do not mean any harm, Miss Beckingham, but these questions you are asking stem from baseless accusations on both accounts. I have long since buried any ill will I might have briefly held against Alastair Drummond, and Gordon will soon see that his accusations are unfounded, as well. It would be a shame if you held the conversation you overheard against either of us."

Before I could say anything, Samuel Rigby tipped his brown bowler hat and hurried up the lawn towards the castle, leaving me alone.

12

D inner was a quiet affair.

Lord and Lady Drummond remained upstairs, taking their supper separately from the rest of the household. Gordon did the same. Meanwhile, in the dining room downstairs, Sherborne Sharp took up a conversation at the far end of the table with Mr. Rigby, which Vivian Barry interrupted often. And Charles sulked quietly over his plate, probably still distressed that he had found himself in the midst of yet another murder investigation.

I spoke only with my mother, listening to her recounting of how the Drummonds were doing on the first day without their son.

The quiet meal was interrupted only once by the arrival of a stranger, a middle-aged man dressed in tall boots and outdoor clothes. He came into the dining room just as the final course was served and cleared his throat.

"Excuse me," he said. "I am Mr. Kentworth, the estate manager."

Sherborne was so deep in conversation with Samuel Rigby that it took the two of them a moment to realize the newcomer was trying to get their attention.

"I believe Lord Drummond mentioned a hunt to you all upon your arrival," Mr. Kentworth said, looking around the room in search of some kind of recognition. "Under the circumstances, he will be unable to accompany you, and so I have been summoned to the castle and asked to do so. I will be heading out early morning just before dawn, and you are all welcome to join me."

There was something absurd in the suggestion that we should go about our leisure activities as if a death hadn't just recently taken place in our midst. Still, it seemed that Lord Drummond remained determined to try and create as normal an atmosphere for us all as possible. I supposed in such a tense situation, it might even be wise to try and keep everyone busy and our minds off more unpleasant matters.

Samuel Rigby had a few questions for the estate manager about where everyone would meet and where they would be going, but I didn't pay any attention. I had no desire to join the hunt and even if I did, it was rather clear the invitation extended only to the gentlemen.

When Mr. Kentworth left after reminding everyone to meet him in front of the castle before sunrise, Sherborne turned to Charles and shook his head. "Hunting seems like a dangerous activity when one of us might be a murderer, does it not?"

"You don't really think that, do you?" Vivian asked, laying a hand on her chest.

Sherborne shrugged. "I'm not sure what to think. I

just know I wouldn't want whoever hurt Alastair to be walking around with a gun."

"If the person wanted to kill you, Sherborne, I'm sure they would have by now," I said.

The entire table turned to me, eyes wide. My mother gasped. "Alice. That is hardly appropriate."

But Sherborne only laughed. "No, she is right, Lady Ashton. And really, her words are a comfort to me."

"How so?" my mother asked, still nudging my knee reproachfully under the table.

Sherborne puffed out his chest and smiled. "Because I am the most aggravating person here in the castle. If the murderer hasn't killed me yet, then it has to mean there isn't a killer at all."

Charles snapped his attention from his plate to Sherborne. "You believe Alastair killed himself, then?"

Vivian hit her brother's arm with her closed fist. "This is not something we should be speculating about. It is crude."

"I suppose I should have said 'there isn't a killer *in this house*,'" Sherborne amended. "If the murderer has not come after me then it means he must be from outside the castle."

"Or she," I offered.

The table turned to me again as though they were all individually shocked I knew how to speak at all.

"We do not know the killer was a man," I said.

"I can't imagine a woman doing something like that," my mother said, wrinkling her nose.

Sherborne looked down the table at me, winking when no one else was paying attention. "I don't know. I've known a number of women who could be capable of such a thing."

I couldn't help but notice that Samuel Rigby turned his gaze to me, as well. I put my head down and avoided joining the conversation until everyone retired to their rooms for the evening.

~

THE MEN WERE GONE by the time I woke up. Off to hunt. Or rather, *shoot at the clouds,* like my father always said.

So, I readied slowly. With no plans to leave the property, I put on a simple cotton dress. It was mauve with small embroidery around the white collar and the sleeves, but otherwise it fell in a straight line to my knee with no other adornment. The plain outfit seemed appropriate for the somber situation at the castle. I paired the dress with brown shoes.

My mother had wanted me to share her room, but I had insisted we would be fine. So, when I walked into the dining room for breakfast, she visibly sighed with relief, presumably pleased that I had not been murdered in my sleep.

Vivian Barry was already there, sipping on a steaming cup of tea.

"Good morning, Alice," Vivian said, drawing out the chair next to her. "Sit with me, won't you?"

"How did you sleep?" I asked, nodding to each of them.

"I don't think I slept a wink," Vivian said. "It was impossible. What with what happened last night. I couldn't stop thinking I heard movement in the halls."

My mother agreed, explaining that a branch from a nearby tree hit her window and nearly sent her running into the corridor screaming.

"And when the gentlemen left this morning," Vivian said, rolling her eyes. "Or rather, in the middle of the night."

"They woke me up, too," my mother said. "I thought there was a stampede moving through the castle."

I nodded in agreement, though, truth be told, I had slept like a dream. Despite everything that had happened in the castle since our arrival, I didn't stir once.

Breakfast was a simple meal of bread and fruit as well as some kind of sausage I didn't fully recognize, and then we all moved into the largest sitting room.

Since our arrival at the castle, Vivian had mostly conversed with her brother and Samuel Rigby, and my mother spent her time with Lady Drummond. So, once we were all in the same room together alone, we realized very quickly we had little to discuss. It wasn't long before my mother broke away to check on the Drummonds and did not return for a long while.

"Your mother is kind to tend to Lord and Lady Drummond the way she has," Vivian said.

Considering I had no interest at all in talking with the bereaved parents, I had to agree. "She is the kindest person I know."

Vivian smiled and then looked towards the cold fireplace. If it was lit, it would give us something to do aside from stare at one another in uncomfortable silence. However, it wasn't, and neither of us seemed eager to jump to the task of summoning a servant to build a fire.

I considered excusing myself and going upstairs to get

into Alastair's room to search it myself, but even with the men out of the house, there was still too much movement. Besides, I didn't know if Sherborne had already searched Alastair's room yet. I would have asked him that morning had they not left for the hunt so early.

The police seemed to think the one valuable item missing from Alastair's room was important. And it made sense. A thief would usually steal more than one item, so either the item had sentimental value to the murderer or the thief was caught in the middle of the crime and killed Alastair to keep him quiet.

The image of Sherborne hunched over in my mother's room flashed in my mind.

I didn't trust Sherborne Sharp, but I couldn't quite imagine him as a killer. Still, it would be dangerous not to keep an eye on him. The deceased had something stolen from his room, and Sherborne was a confirmed thief.

Or could the one item that was stolen have something to do with Samuel Rigby's daughter? I couldn't imagine what it would be, but based on the conversation I'd overheard between Gordon and Samuel, Alastair had been at least loosely involved with Samuel's daughter. Could the item have had some sentimental value to Samuel? Maybe it was an item of his daughter's that Alastair had kept over the years? It was a stretch, but something worth looking into.

Still, none of that explained Alastair's final words about a weeping woman in white.

Had that been the nonsensical ramblings of a dying man or was it a clue?

My mother swept into the sitting room in a flurry, dropping onto the sofa cushion next to me and laying a piece of paper out on the coffee table. She was breathing hard like she was out of breath.

"Are you all right?" I asked.

"Oh, yes, yes," she said, patting my knee. "I've just come from Lady Drummond's room. She was rearranging some of her furniture."

"Rearranging her furniture?" Vivian asked. "Shouldn't the staff take care of that?"

"And why now?" I asked. "It seems an odd time to redecorate."

My mother shook her head, voice low. "She is beside herself with grief, so anything I can do to keep her mind busy, I will do."

She put pen to paper and began writing a letter. "Though, I did need to pull myself away to write a letter to send home."

"To Papa?" I asked.

"He needs to know what is going on here." Then, she looked up at me, her eyes betraying the tiniest hint of nerves. "He needs to know there is a possibility we might not be home when we said we would be."

Vivian gasped. "Do you really think this investigation could take three more days?"

"It is best to be prepared," my mother said, smiling to comfort both me and Vivian.

She began to write, the scratch of her pen on the stationary the only sound in the room until Vivian sighed and dropped her head back on the sofa, a hand pressed to her forehead. "I just cannot believe anyone would do such a thing to Alastair. He seemed like such a friendly man."

"Beloved, according to his parents," my mother added.

Vivian nodded, her blonde curls bouncing. "He had such a good temperament. Very charming."

Despite the generous picture so many people painted of Alastair, I couldn't help wondering whether he made such a good impression on everyone. People below him, people he had no cause to be charming to might have glimpsed a different side of him.

I noticed the skinny housemaid, Hester, lingering nearby with a fresh tray of tea. Deciding to test my theory, I caught the girl's eye and signaled her to come closer.

"Hester, isn't it?" I greeted her.

"Yes, Miss," she answered nervously. She was probably unused to being addressed by the guests, unless they needed something.

"Have you worked here at the castle for very long?" I asked.

"Going on five years, Miss," came the response.

"Then I suppose you must have known young Mr. Drummond very well, having served his family for that long," I said. "Tell us, what sort of employer was he? Was he liked by the household staff?"

"Oh, everyone respected him, Miss. He was quite generous and fair-minded."

I noted that being respected and generous wasn't necessarily the same thing as being liked, but held my tongue on that.

"I was right then," Vivian said. "I knew he was a kind sort of person."

"He was indeed, Miss," the maid agreed softly. "And

he was thoughtful. Even when I first came to work here, he took notice of me and remembered my name."

"That was good of him," my mother said. Then she nodded to the tea. "Thank you for the fresh pot."

Apparently, the girl didn't recognize this as a dismissal, because she lingered still, as if there were something more on her mind.

"Young Mr. Drummond was terribly clever," she volunteered. "I heard it said that he hardly had to study at all to pass his exams at Oxford. He knew a great deal about the history of the castle and about the oldest buildings at the near village, as well. It is rare for a man to be clever, good, and kind, but Mr. Drummond was all three."

Briefly, her face took on a far away expression, as she recalled the many virtues of her former employer. When her expression cleared again, her eyes came to rest on me, and I was startled by the sudden resentment in them. What could the young woman possibly have against me? Surely, she did not blame me for Alastair's sad fate?

Before I could attempt to pry any further information out of her, we were interrupted by the arrival of a plain faced, older woman in a dark dress, who ducked her head in through the doorway. Her straight posture and stern expression signified her position of authority as clearly as the ring of keys dangling from a belt at her waist. I seemed to recall Lady Drummond having introduced her as the housekeeper, at some point.

"Hester," the woman said sharply, obviously displeased to see the maid shirking her work to engage in conversation. "Get back to your duties, girl."

The maid started guiltily, and hurried from the room. That brief flash of resentment I had seen was gone from her eyes, replaced by a meek bearing as she disappeared through the doorway.

The housekeeper's gaze took in the rest of us and her demeanor immediately became respectful. "I hope Hester was not disturbing you ladies with her idle chatter?"

"My daughter was just asking the girl a few questions," Mama answered. "She was not disturbing us at all."

The housekeeper nodded, looking relieved. "I'm glad to hear it. I'm afraid none of the staff are quite themselves at this time. Poor Mr. Drummond was popular with all of the servants and everyone, especially the young female staff, are unnerved by recent events."

"Of course," Mama said with a gracious nod. "It is only natural."

As soon as the housekeeper had left, Vivian leaned forward. "Had someone not come to fetch her, I'm not sure that silly girl would ever have left," she said, showing a hint of amusement. "I think she may have had something of a fancy for her handsome employer."

I usually would have joked with Vivian, but I was too distracted by the memory of Hester's expression before we were interrupted. What had crossed the housemaid's mind to make her look at me so darkly?

Had Gordon's accusation of me having something to do with Alastair's murder made the rounds of the household staff? Did she suspect me?

Our conversation had been private to the best of my knowledge, but then again, I had eavesdropped on a conversation the day before. It was quite an easy thing to do, so perhaps someone had overheard Gordon's theory and shared it.

While I was lost in thought, my mother finished writing her letter in a matter of minutes and went back upstairs to be with the Drummonds. With Vivian becoming engrossed in a book Samuel Rigby had recommended to her the night before, I was left alone.

Thinking about what the household staff might believe happened to Alastair gave me an idea, and on a whim, I excused myself and went in search of the housekeeper. It seemed to me I might gain something by further conversation with her. After all, who better knew the goings on of a great house than its servants?

My SEARCH DIDN'T last long. I found the housekeeper overseeing a maid, possibly a new girl, who looked even younger than Hester. The maid was working in the entryway with a broom and dustpan, cleaning up the debris that had blown in under the large wooden door in the night.

As soon as she heard my footsteps behind her, the older woman murmured some final instructions to the girl and then stepped away to face me.

"Miss Beckingham?" she asked, thin gray eyebrows raised.

I smiled. "I'm sorry. I don't remember your name."

"Mrs. Jameson." Her lips were pressed together firmly, and I could tell she allowed little time for distractions or frivolous chatter.

"Hello, Mrs. Jameson." I dragged my hand aimlessly

across the wooden top of a table against the wall. It was perfectly dusted, each decoration and frame shining. "Do you have a moment to speak with me?"

Her brows knitted together. "I stay very busy throughout the day, but I could spare a second if you need me for something, Miss Beckingham."

"I can tell you are busy," I said. "This castle is immaculate."

Mrs. Jameson offered a small smile, straightening her shoulders slightly. "It is a grand place to work, but maintaining a castle like Druiminn is not without its challenges." Then her eyes suddenly widened, as if she realized that her words might be applied to the present situation and the recent death. "I meant in terms of the work, of course," she added hastily.

"I know what you meant," I said. "But I'm sure the current situation is also a challenge, in its own way. I'm referring, of course, to the events of two nights ago."

Her expression was apprehensive. She glanced back at the young maid working nearby, as if to be sure the girl wasn't listening.

"Difficult and tragic," she said with a shake of her head. "It is too horrible to comprehend."

"Absolutely," I agreed. "Had I not seen it with my own eyes, I might not have believed it."

Mrs. Jameson looked at me with new interest. "Pardon my asking, Miss, but you were the one to find him?"

I nodded. "Unfortunately, yes. Another guest and I overheard Alastair stumbling down the hallway. By the time we found him, he was already beyond help."

Her eyes glazed over, and she shook her head. "I can't

believe something like that could take place in this house. And to such a kind family."

"You enjoy working for the Drummonds, then?" I asked.

Concern flared in her eyes, and I smiled. "I would not tell your secret if you admitted you didn't love it. Believe me, you would not be the first person to dislike their employer."

"Oh, but I do enjoy it," she said, lifting her chin. "I take pride in my work, and Lord and Lady Drummond appreciate my efforts. That is all I can ask for."

"Absolutely. From what little I know of the family, they do seem very warm."

Mrs. Jameson nodded, and then looked back over her shoulder as though she expected one of the family members to be standing behind her. "Well, Miss Beckingham, I'm afraid I should really be getting back to work."

"Wait," I said a touch too quickly.

Mrs. Jameson turned back to me, eyebrows raised. "Yes?"

"I only wanted to ask you," I said, stepping forward and lowering my voice. "Well, I wanted to ask about what you may or may not have seen the night that Alastair – I mean, young Mr. Drummond – was murdered?"

"I already talked with the police," she said. "I told them what I know."

"And I wondered whether you wouldn't share it with me?" I asked. "I know I am no match for the actual detectives, but since I was the first person to find Alastair, I find myself a bit connected to his death. I would love nothing more than to help put the pieces together in any way I can."

Mrs. Jameson's thin lips pressed together so tightly they looked pale. "I appreciate your desire to help, but I don't know what Lord and Lady Drummond would think if I were caught gossiping about the tragedy."

"I understand," I said. "But this would not be gossip. It would simply be sharing facts about what transpired."

Mrs. Jameson twisted her mouth to the side, looking torn.

"I came to you because you have the charge of most of the servants in this house. If anyone were to know anything vital about what happened, my guess is that it would be you."

I could tell immediately that my flattery would pay off. A shine came to Mrs. Jameson's face, and she held herself straighter, prouder.

"Well, that is true," she admitted. "I overhear most of what goes on in the castle."

"And did you happen to overhear anything interesting the night of Alastair's death?"

She frowned. "Unfortunately, no. There were so many new guests staying in the castle and so much extra work to do that I hardly had a second to myself. I ran around all afternoon and evening overseeing guest room preparation and the washing and drying of bed linens. On a normal day, I might have been more mindful of my surroundings, but because of the circumstances, I was in a tizzy."

"Understandable," I said, trying to hide my disappointment. "And that is what you told the police?"

"Yes. I explained my duties for the day and then they asked me whether Mr. Drummond had any enemies—

anyone who could be angry with him or would want him dead."

She paused, staring at me blankly.

I nearly burst with the question. "And what did you say?"

She shrugged her shoulders. "I told them that the deceased was an upstanding young man who was well-liked and respected. Of course, I made no mention of the silly rumors that have been spreading around the castle."

"Rumors?"

She nodded, lips pursed. "Oh, yes. Certain footmen and housemaids have been babbling nonsense about a ghost and the castle being haunted."

I remembered Gordon's claims about Alastair's final words. They had been about the castle's resident ghost—the weeping woman dressed in white. Did this mean news of his final words had made it to the staff?

"I have been employed here for three years now," Mrs. Jameson said firmly. "And believe me, I would know if the castle was haunted. I've been in every corner of this place and have never seen or heard anything supernatural."

"Yes, I'm sure," I said. "Old buildings such as this one are always rumored to be haunted."

"Yes. It's a lot of nonsense," she said, shaking her head.

"However, I wonder—"

Mrs. Jameson raised a brow, and I smiled. "Not about ghosts, of course."

She relaxed.

"I only wonder whether you know anything about the friendship between the Drummonds and Samuel Rigby."

"Mr. Rigby has long been a friend of the family," she said. "Beyond that, I know very little."

"Did you know he had a daughter?"

She glanced over her shoulder again and then nodded. "Yes, I've heard of her, though I never met her. She passed away before I came to work at the castle."

My heart sank. "You were not here when Alastair was involved with Mr. Rigby's daughter?"

"I have no knowledge about the two of them ever being together, but no, I was not here in those days," she said. "That would have been Mrs. Brown, the previous housekeeper."

I quickly ran through the maids in my mind. The only one I knew by name was Hester, and she had already told me that she had been with the family for five years, which was longer than Mrs. Jameson. So, I could question her, though her obvious affection for Alastair might cloud any facts she had about his involvement with Mr. Rigby's daughter. A few of the older maids might know something, so I could ask them. Though, rumors would likely start to circulate if I ran around asking every maid about Alastair's death. And the last thing I wanted was more suspicion being laid on me. Gordon's accusation was likely unfounded and made in the heat of the moment, but I didn't need any other reason for him to suspect me of anything.

"Mrs. Brown served the family loyally for many years," Mrs. Jameson continued. "In fact, when she retired, the family couldn't quite part with her and put her up in a cottage on the edge of the property."

My attention snapped back to Mrs. Jameson. "Mrs. Brown still lives nearby?"

She nodded. "A short ride past the stables, actually. We don't see her often, but she comes up to the servant's hall occasionally. Likes to keep informed of what goes on here at the big house, I suspect."

"And did the police talk with her?" I asked.

"I'm not sure."

"If there was anyone who would know about any longheld family secrets, surely it would be Mrs. Brown," I said feverishly.

Mrs. Jameson's eyes narrowed, and I realized I'd become too excited. "I don't know about any secrets," she said sharply. "But I am sure if the police needed anything from Mrs. Brown, they would have gone to see her. Anyway, the authorities seem to have all in hand. I'm told they believe the murder was committed by a burglar, which seems like a sensible explanation to me. Several windows in the house were left open that night, including poor Mr. Drummond's, and also a smaller window in the back of the kitchen. It is hardly ever used, so I have no reason to believe anyone on my staff opened it during the day."

I did not want to upset Mrs. Jameson, so I did not point out that anyone could have propped open the window for any number of reasons. I also didn't tell her that it was unlikely a burglar would climb through a kitchen window and then specifically go upstairs into a bedroom in the middle of the night to steal from and attack a sleeping Alastair Drummond. Especially since the only item missing in the entire house was something from Alastair's room. If the murderer had the ability to climb to and from Alastair's room specifically, then they would not have need of a kitchen window. And if they did use the kitchen window, then they would have stolen other things from the house.

Evidently feeling she had shared her mind fully enough, Mrs. Jameson took a few steps back. "I must be getting back to work now, Miss Beckingham."

"Thank you for your time."

She pursed her lips together, and I knew I would not be getting any more information from Mrs. Jameson over the course of my stay in the castle. Though, thanks to her telling me about Mrs. Brown, hopefully I would soon have all the information I needed.

13

I took only enough time to change into my riding clothes and then I rushed out of the house, crossing the sweeping back lawn towards the stables.

Even though the police said we were allowed to move freely about the property, I still felt as though I was doing something forbidden. With everything that was going on in the castle, I knew I should have left word with my mother of where I was going, but I didn't want her to ask any questions or forbid my going off on my own.

I needed to talk with Mrs. Brown.

I had a feeling Alastair Drummond was less beloved by some than his family and admirers believed, but I could not prove that without knowing more about the history between Alastair and Samuel Rigby. And I hoped Mrs. Brown would be able and willing to tell me more.

With the men gone for the day, I expected the stables to be empty, but when I pulled open the door, I found a boy who looked about fifteen years old standing in the back stall with the white mare I had ridden my first day at

the castle. I hadn't seen him around the stable yard
before. He looked up as I entered.

"Sorry, I didn't expect anyone to be here," I said.

"And I didn't expect anyone until the gentlemen
returned from their hunt," he said, brushing the mare's
back leg with a stiff brush.

"Are you one of the stable boys?"

He nodded and backed out of the stall, closing the
wooden door behind him. "I am. Were you looking to
ride?"

"I was." I tipped my head to the white mare. "I prefer
the mare."

"She is the tamest of the bunch," he said, grabbing a
saddle from the wall behind him and nodding for me to
follow him. "A good choice."

Once the horse was ready, the boy held out his hand
to help me up, but then hesitated. "You aren't planning to
leave the property, are you?"

"No," I said. "The police have made it clear that is not
allowed."

"All right, good. I have been instructed to monitor
who comes and goes from the stables, and if anyone is
planning to leave, I'm supposed to alert Lord
Drummond."

"Well, there is no need to alert anyone," I said with a
smile. "I am simply going for a ride to clear my head and
get out of the castle."

Contented with my answer, the boy helped me onto
the horse and sent me on my way.

The animal was broad and strong beneath me and it
took me a few minutes to grow accustomed to riding her
again. I pulled on the reins in the direction where Mrs.

Jameson said Mrs. Brown's cottage would be, but the mare was reluctant to follow my lead, moving instead back towards the castle.

"No, girl," I grunted, pulling harder on the reins. "This way."

The horse shifted course slightly but not enough to make any difference. She was headed straight for the woods that marked the edge of the property on one side.

I looked over my shoulder to see the stable boy watching me from the door, his hands on his hips. He was too far away to see my face, but I hoped he could tell by my actions that I was doing my best to correct the horse. I didn't want him running inside to tell anyone that I had taken a horse from the stables. My hope was to meet with Mrs. Brown and then return to the castle before anyone knew any differently.

"Please," I begged, kicking the horse's sides with my heels and tugging on the reins. "There will be a juicy carrot in it for you if you just do as I say."

I didn't know whether the horse could understand me or whether I had simply annoyed her enough that she began following my instruction, but finally, she turned around and began trotting off in the direction of the cottage as though she had been excited about the idea from the start.

When I looked back to the stable, the boy was gone, and I prayed he hadn't gone into the castle already.

But to avoid discussing my ride with anyone, I kicked the mare's sides again and encouraged her to move faster, clinging to her back as she cantered across the hilly landscape.

The countryside truly was beautiful. Green

stretched as far as the eye could see, and even under the overcast sky, the land seemed to glow as though it produced its own light and did not require the sun at all.

After riding awhile and enjoying the sights around me, I began to wonder whether I hadn't gone too far.

Mrs. Jameson had not been specific about the whereabouts of the cottage, and I did not know the area well enough at all to know when I had moved beyond the bounds of the estate. So, I slowed the horse down and began scanning the horizon in every direction, searching for the only landmark I knew to expect.

Just when I began to feel I had certainly gone too far, and I should turn back, I spotted a smoke cloud rising from between the trees.

I clicked my tongue and then, when that didn't work, pulled on the reins to encourage the horse towards the smoke. Slowly, I saw the cottage reveal itself from between the trees.

It was a quaint property. A small stone building that looked to be a similar age to the castle. There was a garden in front filled with various vegetables and greens and a little well on the front lawn. I wrapped the horse's reins around a low-hanging tree branch, straightened my dress, and moved towards the door.

It opened before I even knocked, and a short, white-haired woman appeared.

"Who are you?"

"Hello," I said, my voice high with surprise. "My name is Alice Beckingham. I'm a guest of the Drummond family."

The woman didn't seem at all comforted by my

announcement, and closed her door slightly until I could only see a portion of her face. "What do you want?"

I wasn't sure what exactly I expected to find at the cottage, but I was not prepared to have to talk my way into the woman's house. Still, I had navigated enough uncomfortable conversations over the last two days to at least have some idea of how best to handle this discussion. I folded my hands behind my back and smiled sadly.

"I'm sure you have heard about the tragic death of Mr. Drummond the other night?" I asked.

Mrs. Brown nodded. "The police spoke with me, yes."

So the police had been here. That seemed like a good sign. Assuming the woman told them everything she knew—including whatever information she might have about Samuel Rigby and Alastair's connection—then the police might be well on their way to solving the crime. Assuming, of course, Gordon was right and Mr. Rigby was the murderer.

"I am just a friend of the family. Truthfully, I don't know them very well, but I spoke with Mrs. Jameson," I said, raising my eyebrows in a question. Mrs. Brown nodded, letting me know she recognized the name. "And she told me that you would know more than anyone about the family's history."

There was a moment where I didn't think Mrs. Brown would give in to flattery. I thought the eccentric old woman might slam the door in my face. But then, she opened the door a bit more and took a step out onto the porch, allowing me to see her silk slippers and matching house gown. Clearly, she had not been expecting visitors.

"Do you have questions for me?" she asked.

"If you wouldn't mind."

She studied me for a moment and then stepped aside, ushering me into her home.

The house was just as small on the inside as it appeared from the outside, but Mrs. Brown kept it nice and tidy. She had two chairs in her sitting area, arranged around the fireplace, and a rickety table in the middle of the kitchen. The small space was sweltering because of the fire, and I could already feel a sweat breaking out on my forehead, but I still accepted the seat she offered me only a few feet from the hearth.

Mrs. Brown, like Mrs. Jameson, seemed to be a no-nonsense kind of woman. I was sure that had a lot to do with the fact that they were both experienced at being in charge of a large household staff. They had to command respect.

"What is your interest in the Drummond family?" she asked.

I told Mrs. Brown that I was both curious and concerned about Alastair's death. Having been the one to find him as he was dying, I couldn't push the questions out of my mind. I needed to do my best to have them answered.

"And have you found the answers you are looking for?" she asked.

"Not all of them," I admitted. "That is why I'm here to see you. Mrs. Jameson said you worked with the family for many years."

"I did," she said. Then, she narrowed her eyes. "And that is why I have and will remain loyal to them."

"And I would never wish to tarnish that long history

of loyalty. I only wonder whether you know anything about the Drummond's friendship with Samuel Rigby."

"Ahh," she said, tipping her head back and drumming her fingers on her knees. "Yes, their connection has gone back many years. Lord and Lady Drummond have always been fond of Samuel Rigby and his work."

I nodded, waiting for her to elaborate, but she stared at me with a quiet kind of intensity that let me know I would have to work for any information I got from her.

"And what of their children?"

Immediately, her mouth quirked up in a pleased smile. "It seems you have stumbled upon a bit of information before coming to me."

"I have been thorough."

She smiled and folded her hands in her lap, preparing to tell a story. I wondered how often people came out to the cottage to visit her. Based on her leisure clothes, it didn't seem she expected guests often. Maybe I was the first person in awhile—aside from the police—to care what she had to say. If so, I hoped it meant she would tell me all she knew.

"Gordon Drummond was always reserved. He was not one to mingle much with others or form new friendships. Young Alastair, however, was friendly and sociable since he was a young child. So, when Samuel Rigby began visiting regularly with his daughter in tow, she and Alastair became fast friends."

"And did they become anything more?" I asked.

"That depends who you ask," she answered coyly. "According to the parents, there was no such connection. Lady Drummond is a kind woman, but she has standards for her son, and the daughter of a then-struggling writer would not have been her first choice."

I leaned forward. "And if I had asked Alastair or Mr. Rigby's daughter?"

She arched an eyebrow. "A different story would emerge."

I was desperate for information and decided to be frank. "I overheard Gordon say that Samuel's daughter and Alastair may have been lovers."

Mrs. Brown pursed her lips, looking displeased that someone had beat her to the twist in the story, and then nodded. "I cannot say for certain how far the relationship went, but I can tell you that Jenny Rigby cared for Alastair Drummond deeply. Despite his family's protestations, she very much believed the two of them would end up together."

"And how did you know that?" I asked.

"Members of household staff are often overlooked or expected to silently move through the house without really paying attention to much, but we see more than people know," she said. "I spotted the two of them together in quiet corners often enough to know something was going on. And having been a young woman myself once, I recognized the look of love on the girl's face."

I had a feeling Mrs. Brown would not have been so forthcoming had she still worked for the Drummonds. But now that her working days were done, she was ready to let loose the secrets she had been holding.

"And then Jenny died?" I prodded.

She frowned, her eyes turning downwards. "She did.

The poor girl grew sick and died rather quickly. It was a shock to everyone."

I shook my head, confused. "She became ill?"

Mrs. Brown nodded.

"Then why would Samuel Rigby have ever believed Alastair was responsible for her death?" I asked. "He could not purposefully cause her to contract a disease."

"A woman with a broken heart is more prone to illness," she said simply. "Or, at least, that is what many people believed."

"Alastair broke her heart?"

Mrs. Brown leaned forward and looked up at me from beneath unkempt eyebrows. "Between you and me, Alastair's intentions with the girl had never been honorable, and when she realized he had no intention of marrying her, she descended into a terrible melancholy."

I sighed. "I'm sorry, Mrs. Brown, but do you really believe she died of a broken heart?"

The old woman wrinkled her nose. "No. To me, it is most likely she contracted the influenza. It was especially bad that year and the girl had always been on the sickly side."

I nodded, thinking through everything. Even if the reasoning behind the claim that Alastair had caused Jenny's death was faulty, that wouldn't matter. Samuel Rigby would have been beside himself with grief and not thinking logically. If he bought into the idea that Jenny died of a broken heart, then he would certainly hate the man who had purposefully deceived his daughter. Perhaps, he would hate the man enough to wait for the perfect opportunity to murder him. Even if he had to wait years for that opportunity.

"Clearly, I gave you something to think about," Mrs. Brown said, leaning back in her chair and folding her hands in her lap.

"You did," I said. "Would you care to give me even more to think about?"

The woman raised an eyebrow, intrigued.

"Do you believe Samuel Rigby could have killed Alastair in revenge?"

She twisted her mouth to one side, making the wrinkles in her face even more apparent, and then sighed, her head bobbing back and forth. Finally, she settled on an answer. "You want to know what I think? I think there are more people than even I know who had reason to hate Alastair Drummond."

Mrs. Brown did not ask me if I wanted a refreshment or to stay for a meal. When she decided the conversation was over, she stood up and led me to the door. I thanked her for her time, but she did not respond. Instead, the moment I stepped outside, she began to close the door.

The last thing I heard before it clicked shut was a sudden warning she tossed at my back, "Mark my words. There's still darkness lingering up at that castle. Were I you, I would not return to it."

Before I could ask for further details, she closed the door behind me and I heard the sound of a lock sliding into place.

14

I untied my horse and climbed into the saddle,
already feeling much more at home atop the
animal than I had two days before. The mare, it
seemed, had taken to me, as well. Or perhaps she was
simply eager to get back to the stables. Either way, she
headed in that direction immediately and with little
direction from me.

By my estimation, we were halfway between the
cottage and the stable when I heard a thundering sound
coming from the woods on our right. My horse seemed
skittish, side-stepping the trees slightly and shaking her
head. I kicked her sides to encourage her onward, but she
maintained pace. I didn't know if this was a good sign
or not.

I glanced over my shoulder as we rode, listening as
the sound grew nearer. I noted the crunch of leaves and
twigs.

Someone was coming.

I had only just reached the realization and was doing

my best to get the mare away from the area when a horse broke through the tree line in front of us.

I pulled back on the reins hard enough that the horse turned her head, though she did not change course. If anything, she moved towards the other horse.

And then I understood why.

"Alice?"

The rider was Gordon Drummond. His round face was flushed from the wind, and his red hair stuck up in every direction. Dirt was splattered across his boots and the legs of his horse.

"What are you doing here?" he asked.

"I came out for a ride," I said quickly as four more horses with riders came out of the trees behind him. Mr. Kentworth, the estate manager was in the lead.

"Is that Miss Alice?" Charles Barry asked, clearly puzzled.

"The very same," Sherborne Sharp said, riding up next to Gordon and pulling his horse to a stop at a diagonal. A single dark eyebrow was raised.

"I didn't realize you all were out this direction," I admitted. "I just rode out for some fresh air."

"If you had wandered much further, you might have found yourself part of the hunt," Sherborne said with a loud laugh. "You are nearly on the hunting field."

Given the murderer still on the loose, Sherborne's comments struck me as inappropriate and made me uncomfortable, but I simply smiled along with him.

"Lucky for me I was heading back to the castle now," I said, pulling on the reins and trying to navigate around Gordon's large beast.

"A gentle tug is all it takes to lead her," Gordon said,

demonstrating for me on his own animal. "And we are heading back, too."

My mare had been, after all, a little difficult today, so I refrained from pointing out that I knew how to handle a horse.

"We will all ride together," Sherborne said, stretching his arms out wide as if he wanted us—horses and all—to join him in a group embrace.

Samuel Rigby seemed eager to ride ahead, making no eye contact with me, and Charles seemed disinterested either way. That left me trailing just behind Sherborne Sharp and just in front of Gordon Drummond.

"I had not realized you were so fond of the outdoors," Gordon said, urging his horse up next to me.

Whether on purpose or not, Sherborne pulled away, as well, allowing a bit of comfortable space between us so he would not overhear our conversation.

"A lot can change in a day," I said. I immediately regretted the words.

"Indeed, it can," Gordon said softly.

"I'm sorry. That is not what I meant."

He waved away my embarrassment. "We all say things we do not mean."

I stared at the side of his face, wondering if his words perhaps had two meanings. Then, he turned to me, the full force of his green eyes on mine. "Forgive me, Alice."

I looked away, uncomfortable with the emotion in his face. In the few short days I'd spent at Druiminn Castle, I had become comfortable with the surly, disinterested Gordon who cared little what anyone thought. But in front of me now, I could see every emotion from the last couple of days written plainly on his face. He was a grieving man.

"There is nothing to forgive."

He nudged his horse closer to mine. "I accused you of a horrible thing, Alice, and I had no right."

"Your brother had just died," I said, voice low. "I understood then and I understand now. You do not need to apologize."

He sighed. "Please don't be stubborn. Just forgive me."

When I looked up at him now, the emotion was still obvious in his eyes, but he was smiling. I couldn't help but smile in return. "You are forgiven."

His shoulders relaxed and slowly, as we cantered towards the castle, his horse shifted away from mine. Our group moved in a quiet unit, everyone too tired or too lost in thought to speak until we returned to the stables.

Charles Barry groaned as he dismounted just outside the stable doors and handed his reins off to a groom who came running to fetch them. "My legs will be sore for the rest of the week, I think."

"That is surprising, Charles. You seem like the kind of man who would partake in a great deal of physical activity," Sherborne said, clearly teasing.

Charles, however, was oblivious, and puffed up his chest. "I explore the grounds around our home frequently and enjoy a long walk. But it is not often that I find myself on the back of a horse."

Sherborne opened his mouth to make another remark, but Gordon nudged him and shook his head, as Charles drifted away.

I scrambled down from my own mount as the stable boy I had met earlier came to assist me.

I was watching him lead my horse away when Sherborne, who had dismounted by now, moved to stand next to me. "The job is done."

I turned to him, forehead wrinkled. "Excuse me?"

"I snuck into Alastair's room last night," he whispered, after handing off his horse's reins to a servant. He nodded for me to follow him to the castle.

Gordon had emerged from the stable already and hurried off up the path in front of us with Charles, Mr. Kentworth, and Samuel Rigby following behind, so I knew we would not be overheard.

"What did you find?"

"Aside from an open window and some blood stains, nothing," he said with a shrug. "His room looked the same as always."

"You didn't notice anything missing?" I asked, disappointed.

He shook his head. "Nothing obvious. Did you have any luck talking to Gordon?"

"Not yet." Though, since he had just apologized to me about the accusation he made, perhaps I would have another chance to ask him about what was missing from his brother's room.

Suddenly, Sherborne grabbed my arm and pulled me to a stop. "Maybe this is a sign that this investigation should end."

"You don't want to know what happened?" I asked, confused by his change of heart. He had seemed willing enough to help me before.

Sherborne ran a hand through his dark hair, looking more frazzled than I'd ever seen him. His examination of Alastair's room and the sight of those blood stains must have disturbed him more than he let on. The easy, joking figure from just a few minutes ago was gone. "Of course, I want to know, but I think the police will solve this and save us the trouble."

"And what if they don't?"

"Then what makes you think we can do it on our own?" Sherborne held his hands up and took a few steps away from me. "I know you are strangely committed to unraveling this mystery, but I think it looks better for both of us if we let it rest here."

He must have been able to read the confusion on my face because he explained what he was really thinking. "I snuck into his room last night, Alice. Do you know how bad it would have looked if I'd been caught? I can't be seen poking around this investigation."

So that was it. I understood his concern, but I also wanted to know what Sherborne had to hide.

He was Alastair's best friend for years. No one would suspect him of murder. If he was found in Alastair's room, he could easily explain it away as missing his friend or mourning him and no one would think twice. But clearly, Sherborne was nervous, anxious to be done with the investigation, and I had to wonder why.

"Fine," I said. "We are done."

He furrowed his brows. "Are *we*? Or am I?"

"Does it matter?" I asked.

He sighed and lowered his head, looking down his nose at me. "It doesn't look good for you either, Alice. You would be wise to get through this week and then go home. There is no reason to involve yourself further."

It struck me that throughout everything that had happened, Sherborne Sharp had not seemed very deeply moved by his friend's death. Perhaps their friendship had been less about genuine affection, at least on Sherborne's side, and more a matter of convenience. For a man who had admitted his own family's fortunes were failing, maybe it had been necessary for him to cultivate useful acquaintances like Alastair Drummond.

I'd put aside my doubts about him early on, out of desperation. I wanted to investigate Alastair's death, but I didn't know if I could do it on my own. But now Sherborne was encouraging me to drop the investigation. I couldn't help but wonder if he had been involved in some way. Especially as his supposed friendship with the victim had apparently been a rather shallow one. It was just possible that Sherborne was a colder, more calculating figure than I had initially thought.

I remembered what Mrs. Brown had said, that more people than anyone knew had reason to dislike Alastair. Did she know more about the friendship between Alastair and Sherborne than anyone else did? Perhaps Alastair had found out about Sherborne's penchant for theft? If he had caught Sherborne stealing from him and threatened to reveal his secrets, might not Sherborne have concluded that this particular acquaintance had outlived his usefulness?

I didn't know for sure, but as I walked to the castle next to Sherborne, I decided definitively that whatever I did for the remainder of the investigation, I would do alone.

~

MY MOTHER HAD BEEN busy enough tending to the Drummonds that she hadn't noticed my absence. Vivian, too, didn't seem to think anything was amiss when I walked into the castle with the men returning from the hunt. And none of the gentlemen seemed to think it was important enough to mention. All of which I was grateful for.

I returned to my room to dress for dinner. I changed out of my riding clothes and into a blue satin gown with a wide embroidered waist and box collar, a lace headband, and a pair of black pumps.

Everyone had taken their seats and begun to eat when Lord and Lady Drummond made an unexpected appearance at the start of dinner. They both looked pale and thin, but they took their places at the far ends of the table and put on brave faces for their guests.

"Please, eat," Lord Drummond instructed with a sad smile.

Lady Drummond didn't say anything, but my mother stayed near her throughout the meal, winking at me once from across the table.

The guests obeyed and ate, though there was little conversation. Vivian and her brother talked quietly to one another and my mother occasionally whispered in Lady Drummond's ear, but otherwise, the table was silent.

No one knew how to behave in front of the Drummonds. Obviously, they were devastated by the loss of their son, so having any conversation where people would laugh or smile felt disrespectful. Even the servants who were bringing out different courses and filling glasses looked nervous as they flitted around the room.

The red-haired maid, Hester, stared longingly at the

Drummonds as though she wanted to speak with them, though she never did. When she wasn't looking at Lord and Lady Drummond, she turned her eyes to me. A few times, I caught her staring, and she waited a few seconds before looking away. It felt as though she was trying to tell me something, though I didn't know what.

At the end of the meal, Lord and Lady Drummond thanked their guests and then went immediately back upstairs. My mother pulled me into a quick embrace before she followed Lady Drummond.

As soon as I was alone, I scanned the room for Hester. She was standing next to the wall, waiting for the table to clear of guests so she could move in with the other servants and clear the table. But once again, she met my gaze and held it.

I took a step towards her, but that was all I managed before Samuel Rigby moved into my path.

"Miss Beckingham," he said solemnly.

I took a step backwards, surprised by his sudden appearance and that he wanted to speak with me at all after our conversation the day before on the lawn.

"Mr. Rigby." I folded my gloved hands in front of me, fidgeting with the lace at my wrists. "Did you enjoy the hunt today?"

"Are you still investigating Alastair's death?" he asked suddenly, ignoring my question.

My mouth fell open, and I tried to find the words. They came out in a jumble. "I was not—have not been—investigating anything. I only had a few questions for you. That is all."

Samuel pursed his lips together, his mustache twitching at one corner. "Well, as we've already established, I will not be answering any more questions. However, I did wish to mention to you—or to anyone who might be interested in the matter—that there is a portion of the castle rarely travelled by anyone in the household."

I narrowed my eyes. "Lady Drummond offered me a tour the day I arrived."

He nodded. "And there is a room at the far end of the corridor upstairs that leads to another level. A space that has stood unused and forgotten. Centuries' worth of secrets lie up there."

"What are you saying, Mr. Rigby?" I asked, a chill moving down my spine.

He shrugged innocently, smiling and nodding as Vivian Barry passed by us on her way into the sitting room. "I'm simply saying that if anyone was searching for secrets around here, they would be wise to look there. But, of course, you've said you are not searching for anything, so you are probably not interested."

"No, not especially," I said quickly. "But thank you for the information regardless."

He tipped his head and walked calmly into the sitting room, leaving me to wonder what had just happened.

Coming out of my surprised daze, I looked around for Hester again, but she was gone, as were most of the table settings. She would be busy in the kitchens for the rest of the night, and I knew I would have to wait until the morning to speak with her. If she had actually wanted to speak with me at all.

So, I moved into the sitting room and did my best to partake in the conversations happening there. My mind, however, was far above the space that I and my fellow guests inhabited, lingering in a mysterious place on the upper floor.

No one seemed keen to linger in the hall where Alastair had died, so I did not need to wait long after everyone retired to their rooms for the evening to sneak out of my own.

As I slipped out my bedroom door, I wondered at my own boldness. Everything about the information Mr. Rigby had given me spoke of a trap, an ideal opportunity for him, if he was in fact the killer, to lure me to a lonely part of the castle and end my life. And yet, surely he would not be so clumsy, so obvious if he was truly a threat? No, the more I thought back on our brief exchange, the more I wondered if he was trying to give me a hint about someone else. But if that were the case, why would he not simply tell me whatever he knew or suspected? It was this confusion and lack of answers that compelled me to go.

Except for one flickering light every ten paces, the rest of the lamps in the hallway had been doused, plunging everything into murky shadows. I'd brought a small candle from my room, but it did little to dispel the gloom, and I had to place my feet carefully on the floor to avoid stumbling over uneven spots in the stone or tripping over the corners of tables.

In telling me about the secret portion of the castle, Samuel had nodded his head towards the east wing, so I followed that corridor to the end and then found a wooden door that looked different from the others. It was made of a heavier wood with large iron hinges and an iron doorknob.

I turned the knob slowly, wincing when it let out a low squeal—probably from disuse—and then pushed it open.

I was met with the sight of stone steps, the edges soft and rounded from time. I mounted them quickly, pulling the door closed behind me so no one else would see it open and become suspicious.

Immediately, it felt as though I was in a different castle altogether. The stairwell was noticeably cooler than the rest of the house and it smelled damp and earthy, as though I was moving deep into a cellar, rather than walking an upper level.

When I reached the top of the stairs, I held my candle out in front of me, hoping to illuminate the space, but I was met with nothing but blackness.

Instinct caused me to momentarily search for a light before I remembered the castle had no electricity. My small candle would be the only illumination I would find, and I wasn't certain it was enough to see anything.

I took small, careful steps across the stone, noting the thick layer of dust that clouded around my feet with every movement, and swiveled my head from side to side as my eyes adjusted slightly to the darkness.

I began to make out the rough shape of the room. It appeared to be a kind of wide hallway—similar in size to the corridor on the second floor below, but there were no doors leading to connecting rooms or windows allowing in moonlight. Just endless stone walls stretching into the darkness.

As I walked, I kicked loose stones that slid across the

floor and made me jump. Then, there were the skittering sounds not caused by me. I tried not to think about the rats or other animals that might be hiding up here with all of the secrets Samuel Rigby alluded to, but I couldn't help but imagine them. In fact, it was all I could think about.

Until, of course, I saw a flash of movement at the end of the hallway.

It was quick. Nothing more than a whisper of movement. But it had been white.

My heart thundered in my chest, beating against my ribcage until I thought it would burst.

From the moment I'd heard of Alastair's final words, I'd never once considered the possibility that his words about the weeping woman in white could have actually been in reference to the spirit herself.

Now, however, alone in the strange space, she felt more real to me than anything else.

Sadness leached out of the stones, filling me with the grief the woman from the legend must have felt when her heart was broken. I could practically hear her wailing. But rather than run in fear, I stood frozen in the middle of the hallway, staring wide-eyed into the darkness, trying to make out any movement.

Then, a door slammed.

I didn't know where it came from or how far away it was, but it meant I wasn't alone. Whether in the presence of a person or a spirit, I didn't know, but I knew I had to get out of there as soon as possible.

So, throwing all caution aside, I turned and sprinted back in the direction I'd come from.

Except, I hit a wall.

The palms of my hands took most of the impact, but I still stumbled backwards, grunting from the unexpected barrier. Then, I spun around, but I could no longer tell which direction I'd come from.

Had I hit the wall to the right or my left? If I took another step, would I be moving towards the slamming of the door I'd heard or further away?

The only sound seemed to be the rush of blood in my ears.

Then, I heard footsteps.

They were soft at first, quiet enough that I could have mistaken them for the scurrying of a small animal or the wind. But as they grew louder, the sound was too recognizable. Too obvious.

As they grew closer and closer, I shrunk back against the wall, making myself as small as I possibly could.

Suddenly, there was a blaze of light.

I was blinded, overwhelmed by the sudden brightness, and I screamed.

For a moment, I didn't recognize the scream as my own. It sounded so terrified, so foreign.

Then, there were hands on my arms, and I thrashed, trying to pull away. Until I heard his voice.

"Alice, stop! Before you kill us both."

I froze and held a hand to my eyes, trying to shield away some of the light.

The light in front of me shifted, and I saw a silhouette of a tall, narrow man. I looked up at him, blinking from the brightness.

"Gordon?"

He grabbed my arm and yanked me roughly away from the wall, and I screamed again.

15

"Stop thrashing before you fall," he said, holding me against his chest.

"Fall?" My terror had given way to confusion.

Gordon took a few steps backwards, carrying me with him, and then held out his light. The wall where I'd just been standing was illuminated, and I could see a large dark stain on the floor. I leaned down to get a better look, and Gordon pulled me back.

"The floor could give way any moment," he said. "We need to get out of here."

"The floor?"

Gordon kept a firm hand around my arm as he dragged me to the center of the hallway. "This old section of the castle is falling apart. It's been abandoned for years and is little more than a ruin. What are you even doing here, Alice?"

I could see the sunken parts of the floor now. In the dark, I'd thought the floor was rough and uneven, but now I realized it was actually sagging.

I could have fallen to my death.

"What are you doing here?" I asked, pulling as far away from him as his hold on me would allow. "How did you find me?"

"I didn't. Hester did."

I shook my head, confused. "Hester?"

He dragged me a few more steps down the corridor, careful to avoid the worst parts of the floor, and I followed his lead. "I saw her walking towards the door to the stairs, and when I asked what she was doing, she said she saw you come up here. She was going to come get you herself, but I decided to risk my own life instead."

I was still too flustered to fully understand what had happened. I looked back over my shoulder, half-expecting to see the weeping woman in white waiting in the middle of the hallway for me. There was nothing. Just darkness.

"There should be a warning sign or something," I said.

"Ordinarily our guests don't go exploring the castle on their own at night," Gordon said harshly. "And usually there is a sign warning visitors away from this wing. Maybe it was moved during the police investigation. I'm not sure. But we'll definitely be replacing it now that we almost had two deaths in the castle in the same week."

I debated telling Gordon that Samuel Rigby had sent me to this part of the castle. Surely, as a historian and author, he would have known this portion of Druiminn Castle was falling to waste. Still, I couldn't quite believe he would send me to my death on purpose.

But even if he had, I'd vowed to handle the investigation on my own. And Gordon had enough to deal with, clearly, without me offering up my unsolicited theories. So, I stayed quiet and followed him down the stairs.

When we got to the hallway, Hester was nowhere to be found. I was surprised she hadn't waited to make sure we'd made it down safely. But then again, I couldn't exactly blame her. If Gordon had been as angry when he'd left her in the hallway as he was now that we had returned safely, I would have run if I was her, too.

Gordon escorted me all the way down the hallway to my room. He waited until I'd bid him goodnight and closed the door before finally walking away and going back to his own room. I listened to his footsteps grow more and more quiet. And then, eventually, there came the soft thud of his door closing.

∼

I DIDN'T SLEEP.

The brief flash of white I'd seen at the end of the hallway appeared every time I closed my eyes. And the few times I dared to drift to sleep, the woman in white was waiting in my dreams.

So, I pulled a dressing gown tightly around my shoulders and paced my room, waiting for morning. When it finally came, I dressed quickly in a dark blue skirt and cream blouse, and long brown shawl before meeting my mother in the corridor for breakfast.

"Alice," she said, knitting her brows together. "You look exhausted. Are you feeling well?"

"Just nightmares," I said.

I could tell by the sad look in her eyes that she thought my nightmares had something to do with Alastair's death. And in a roundabout way, they did. Though, not in exactly the way she expected.

I didn't tell her about my excursion the night before. About how Samuel had sent me up to the most dangerous part of the castle, possibly so I would die. I didn't tell her because I wasn't yet certain of Samuel Rigby's motives. I needed more evidence.

And when we walked into the dining room for breakfast, I got it.

Hester was frozen in the doorway, eyes wide, clutching a tray of freshly cut fruit. And standing in front of her with a finger pointed at her chest was Samuel Rigby.

As soon as the two of them heard us approach, Samuel backed away and stood tall, gesturing for Hester to continue readying the sideboard for the guests. Hester did just that, though I noticed her face was pale and her hands shook as she worked.

Hester had wanted to speak to me last night after dinner, but Samuel had interrupted her. Then, she had followed me to the stairs that led to the crumbling part of the castle where Samuel had sent me.

For reasons I didn't understand, Hester was trying to warn me of something, and clearly, Samuel didn't want her to.

The Barry siblings arrived for breakfast moments later, followed by Gordon Drummond and then Lord and Lady Drummond. Vivian took the seat next to Samuel, capturing his attention, and my mother moved to greet the Drummonds. At that same moment, Hester reappeared with another pitcher of fresh orange juice.

I stood at once and met her at the sideboard.

"Hester," I whispered, squeezing various fruits as if testing them for ripeness.

The maid turned to me, looking surprised. "Yes, Miss?"

"Thank you for sending Gordon for me last night," I said softly. "I might not have found my way safely out without him."

She pressed her lips together and nodded. "Of course, Miss."

She moved as if trying to leave, but I hissed for her to wait. "Why were you following me? Did you have something to tell me?"

Hester looked nervously over her shoulder, and then shook her head. "It was simple luck, Miss. Good fortune."

"I think it was more than that."

"It wasn't," she said sharply. Then, she glanced towards the table, and I followed her gaze to see Samuel Rigby carefully watching the two of us. Hester snapped her attention back to her work and mumbled under her breath. "It was lucky, but I'm not sure you'll get so lucky again. If you have any concern for your life, you'll stay away from that part of the house."

Before I could say anything, Hester hurried out of the room and didn't come back again.

THE ACTIVITIES available to the guests were growing stale and a general sense of discontent was starting to brew.

Charles Barry looked even more miserable than when he and his sister had arrived, which I didn't think could be possible, and his sister, Vivian, had apparently decided that romancing Samuel Rigby would be the best use of her time.

"Samuel," she said, brushing his shoulder and laughing. "You are too bad. Really, you can't go about saying things like that."

Gordon cleared his throat. "Please, Mr. Rigby. Do share your comment with the rest of us. I could use a laugh."

"No, no. He can't," Vivian insisted, dropping into another fit of giggles.

Samuel Rigby simply pinched his lips together and smiled.

And the morning turned to afternoon much in that manner.

No one seemed to know what to do with themselves. There were books to read, but sitting quietly allowed too much time for thought. And there was talk of going out for some air, but before anyone could gather the energy, the sky opened up, drenching the grounds in rain. After that, Vivian wouldn't hear of muddying her shoes.

After lunch, Gordon retreated to his mother's room where my own mother was still spending most of her time, and Vivian, Samuel, and Charles took up a game of cards. They invited me to play, but I saw a window of opportunity that I could not refuse.

"No, I think I will go check on Mama," I politely declined.

Vivian tried to persuade me, but I remained firm and got up to leave. As I did, I felt eyes on me, though I did not turn to see if they belonged to Samuel. It didn't matter anyway. By the time they finished their game, I would be back.

I heard voices coming from under Lady Drummond's bedroom door as I passed on tip-toe, praying no one would open the door and find me. As soon as I was far enough away that they would not see me, I broke into a run.

A chill moved down my neck and back as I approached the door at the end of the hall, but I ignored it, pulled open the door, and mounted the well-worn steps.

Even though there were no windows in the long hallway, it was easier to see in the daylight. This was mostly due to light filtering through the sizable cracks in the walls and ceiling. As I took in the space for the first time in proper lighting, I was amazed I hadn't fallen through the floor the night before.

I picked my way across the floor carefully, avoiding the low spots where the stones seemed to be slipping, and moved towards where I'd seen the flash of movement the other night. I had no idea if I would find anything. I'd come back here to find out if there was a way to explain the movement I'd imagined seeing up here before.

The further I walked, the more likely it became that I wouldn't find anything. And I had just resigned myself to that very real possibility when I looked up and saw a pale white gown floating in the air.

My heart jumped into my throat, and I fell backwards, scraping my palms on the floor in an instinctual scramble away from the ghost. Then, my mind caught up with my actions.

There was a dress hanging in the air, but there was no one inside of it.

The long white dress was hanging from a hook on the

wall, not floating. And the longer I stared at it, the more I
realized it was just a dress. There was nothing other-
worldly about it at all.

So, taking deep breaths to calm myself, I stood up and
walked towards the gown, looking around to ensure I was
alone.

The dress was pure white, but as I approached, I
could see dark splotches across the hem and the sleeves.
The drops could have been mud, but given Alastair's final
words, I had a strong feeling I knew exactly what they
were.

This dress had been worn by Alastair's murderer.

There was a deep pocket on the side of the dress, and
I dug inside of it for any clue, until I felt a small metal
trinket. I pulled it out and turned it over in my palm.

It was a ring. I slipped it onto my finger and knew
immediately it belonged to a man. Even on my thumb,
the ring was loose. Then, I noticed the setting on the ring
—a gold oval with an elaborate 'D' inscribed in the
center. 'D' for Drummond.

Surely the ring belonged to Alastair Drummond.
Somehow in that moment I knew this was the item that
had been stolen from his room.

Thoughts swirled in my head faster than I could
make sense of them. Why would the murderer steal
something as trivial as Alastair's family ring? And why
dress as the woman in white to murder him?

It seemed to me that whoever had murdered Alastair
had done so for a deep, emotional reason. That was the
only thing that could explain the level of pageantry and
the theft of such a sentimental item.

Then, there was the fact that Samuel Rigby had sent

me to this crumbling attic the night before. Was that because he hoped I would fall through one of the gaps in the floor and die or because he wanted me to see the dress. Or both?

Or, even more sinister, had Samuel planned to attack me up here? Just before I turned and ran into Gordon, I'd heard a door slam shut somewhere in the distance. Had he been the flash of white I'd seen? Had the noise been Samuel coming in to attack? If so, I needed to find that door.

I dropped the ring back in the pocket of the dress and walked further into the abandoned space. I didn't have to go far before I found a door set into the stone.

I pressed my ear to the wood, listening for any hint of movement on the other side. When I heard nothing, I pushed the door open carefully.

It opened onto a small room. And just a few paces away was another door. This one looked more modern like the doors in the rest of the house. Once again, I pressed my ear to it, listening for any sound at all. And when I heard nothing, I opened it again.

This time, however, the door opened onto a bedroom.

There was a small bed in the corner of the room with a warped dresser on the other wall. Simple dark dresses hung in the closet, and I knew immediately I had found my way into the attics where the servants were housed. I had stumbled into a room that undoubtedly belonged to one of the maids.

I'd seen several of the servants using a stairwell on the opposite end of the hallway to get to their rooms at the end of the night, so I knew they slept at this level. But it seemed only one of their rooms connected to the crumbling part of the castle. What I wanted to know now was who slept in this room?

I opened the drawers in the dresser, searching for anything that could help me identify whose room I was in, but there was nothing but neatly folded clothes. Then I moved to the closet, where again, I found nothing. Finally, I pulled back the blankets and knelt down next to the bed, bending low to look underneath it. There, I found a small leather journal.

I slid it out from under the bed and ran my hand across the worn material. Clearly, it was a treasured item. Probably a diary of some kind.

I unwound the strap and flipped it open, and written on the front page was a name: Hester Adair.

I replayed the image of Hester and Samuel that morning. He had been warning her about something, frightening her until she was pale in the face and trembling. Then, when I'd asked about the abandoned part of the castle, she'd looked back at Samuel before warning me not to go up there anymore.

Had Samuel used her room to sneak into the crumbling section of the house to attack me? Perhaps, she discovered the gown somewhere while cleaning and Samuel had somehow convinced the maid to stay quiet about what she'd found? Regardless of how it happened, it was clear Hester was trying to reach out to me. She was trying to tell someone what she knew without putting herself in danger in the process.

Just then, I heard voices outside Hester's door.

As quickly and quietly as possible, I wrapped up the journal, slid it back under the bed, and slipped from the room, going back the way I had come.

I didn't linger to see if anyone came into her room or not. I didn't want to be caught by Samuel if he had decided to use Hester's room to access the ruined wing again.

As I passed by the dress, I considered grabbing it and taking it and the ring with me, but instead, I left them.

Before I touched anything and let Samuel know someone knew his secret, I needed to talk to Hester. I needed to know what she knew.

16

I returned to the group of guests only twenty minutes after I left, but it felt like a lifetime had passed.

I watched Samuel Rigby with renewed focus, searching for any sign of the monster behind the mask. Hester maintained her distance for the rest of the day, not allowing me to see the two of them together or affording me an opportunity to speak with her and organize a time or place we could meet.

Though I tried to refuse several more times, Vivian eventually pulled me into a card game, and I played poorly, barely paying attention to the rules until dinner.

Dinner was another uncomfortable meal. Each time I saw the Drummonds, they seemed to appear more despondent than the time before. No one was at ease in their presence, and as soon as they left, the guests gathered in the large sitting room and seemed to offer a collective sigh of relief.

"Won't you tell us a story, Sam?" Vivian asked, using the nickname she had taken to using in place of Samuel.

"Oh, no one wants to hear another tale," he said modestly.

My mother, who had taken a break from the lord and lady of the house for the evening, clapped her hands and insisted. "Please, Mr. Rigby. I'm sure we would all love a distraction."

"It would be welcome," Charles said, sounding surprisingly eager.

Never one to disappoint his fans, Samuel pulled a chair in front of the fireplace until the flames cast him in silhouette. Only a faint light from the lamps on the wall illuminated the high points of his face, but otherwise, he was cast in shadow. The sight set me on edge.

"History or legend?" he asked, taking a survey of the room.

Legend won without contest, and he twisted his mouth to one side in thought, his blonde mustache twitching, before he lifted his finger and nodded. "I have just the tale."

I did not hear a word of it, however. As soon as Samuel began his story, the servants who had been moving around the house doing their nightly chores stopped to listen, as well.

They began to gather in the doorways and in the dining room within earshot of the story, and I couldn't stop myself from scanning their ranks in search of Hester. Finally, after several minutes, she appeared in the back of the crowd, her red hair catching my eye.

Luckily, my position at the edge of the room allowed me to stand up and slip from the sitting room with relative ease. If Samuel Rigby noticed, there was nothing he could do to stop me without halting his story and drawing the attention and suspicion of the entire room. So, I slipped between the maids and moved to stand next to Hester in the back of the room.

"I know you know something," I said earnestly.

Hester shifted her position and lifted her chin, though I could see the fear in her eyes. Her gaze was locked on Samuel Rigby, and I wanted to tell her she didn't have to be afraid. Though, I didn't know if that was true.

"You can talk to me," I said.

Her jaw clenched, and then she turned to me, her voice so soft I almost couldn't hear her.

"Meet me tonight. In the trees near the stables," she whispered.

My heart began racing, and I moved my hand across the small space between us and grabbed her wrist. "Is this about Alastair?" I asked.

"I've said too much already," she hissed, casting her gaze around to be sure no one had overheard me. "I'll explain everything tonight."

Then, the girl turned on her heel and rushed away.

SITTING through the remainder of the evening, listening to Samuel Rigby regale the guests with story after story, felt like torture. I wanted nothing more than to find Hester and get the answers I so craved. Finally, however, Samuel told the group he was tired and people began to disperse, retiring for the evening.

I walked up the stairs with my mother, her arm wrapped through mine.

"Lord and Lady Drummond have had an update from the authorities, who are confident they are close to solving the case," she said. "There have been a string of break-ins at nearby estates, and they think they may have caught the man responsible."

I nodded and tried to smile convincingly. There was no point in telling her yet that whatever burglar the police may have caught, he was not our killer. "That is welcome news, I'm sure."

"Yes," she said, squeezing my arm. "For the Drummonds and us. We may be able to leave soon."

If all went as planned at my meeting with Hester, then my mother was right. We would be going home very soon.

When I was alone in my room, I didn't change into my nightgown. Instead, I paced the floor, waiting for everyone to go to sleep.

It felt like days since I'd had any true rest, and I could feel exhaustion fraying the edges of my mind, but I pushed through it. I needed to talk with Hester. I needed answers.

I saw through the crack under my bedroom door when the lights in the hallway were doused, and I slipped into a pair of sensible shoes to traverse the uneven ground in the dark.

As I stood up from my bed to continue pacing, however, I glanced out my window and saw a flutter of movement on the lawn. I ran to the glass and looked out, but I did not see anything again.

It was too early for Hester to already be heading to

our meeting location. Unless, of course, she had decided to get there early.

Either way, I was restless in my room and anxious for something to do, so I buttoned my coat and slipped into the hallway. Yet again, the castle was all too easy to sneak out of unseen. The stone floors did not creak in the same way wood floors would have and since the servants slept in the attic, the first floor of the castle was silent.

The night was chilly, and I wrapped my arms around myself as I walked towards the stables.

I tried to stay in the darkness along the base of the house and move from tree to tree to avoid being seen by any of the guests who might still be awake in their rooms. But once I moved beyond the outcrop of trees behind the castle, there was nowhere to hide. Unless, I wanted to cut across the wide expanse of open grass to get to the trees on the other side, I had to simply stay low and move quickly to get to the next stand of trees.

As I walked, I kept looking over my shoulder for Hester, wondering if she would be coming behind me or if I really had seen her leaving for our meeting spot early.

The wind was still, given the amount of open land, but there was enough of a breeze to shake the trees and make it difficult to hear anything beyond my own foot-steps. So, I kept my eyes open and moved quickly.

I made it to the next row of trees and then followed the curve of the wooded area until I was out of sight of the castle and headed down the hill that led to the stables.

Once I saw the stables, I still didn't walk directly towards them. I didn't know where the grooms slept or if they would still be inside caring for the horses, so I decided to stick close to the tree line until I could be certain of truly being alone.

Suddenly, however, there was a break in the trees—a sudden dip in the line where the trees pushed back several feet and a small, shadowy clearing opened up.

And there, in the middle of that clearing, stood the woman in white.

When she looked up at me, I couldn't see her face. Instead, there was a black hole, yawning open as though it was a portal to the other side.

A fear more powerful than anything I'd ever felt tore through me. I stood frozen, pinned to the spot, unable to move or breathe or scream.

Then, she took a step towards me and moved into a small shaft of moonlight breaking through the trees.

And I saw the truth.

~

"Hester."

The word was little more than a breath, a sigh of relief, almost, that the young woman in front of me was human and not a ghost. She was the maid I'd spoken to earlier in the evening, now covered in what appeared to be mud—a crude, hasty disguise.

Her red hair was still tumbling free, and I realized I had interrupted her in the middle of readying herself.

She'd come out to the meeting place early to prepare, to put on her disguise as the weeping woman in white and meet me in the woods. Because that had been her plan, after all. To attack me in the woods. To kill me the same way she had killed Alastair. I could see it all now.

Alastair's final words of a weeping woman in white had been in earnest. In her disguise, he didn't recognize Hester. He'd seen nothing but a pale, haunting figure. But why?

"Why are you doing this, Hester?" I asked.

"Everyone knew you were snooping around, asking questions about Alastair's murder," she said. It was almost strange to hear her voice come from the terrifying figure in front of me. Even though I knew it was Hester, her disguise really was convincing. "You made it all too obvious that you saw yourself as the heroine in a detective novel. Most people thought you were wasting your time. Only I knew how close you were getting."

"You were in the ruined part of the castle the night I went up there," I realized, the true events of that night becoming organized in my mind. "You slammed the door."

"I was going to dispose of the costume," she said, lifting her head and stepping towards me. The same shaft of moonlight that had been on her face caught a glint of silver in her hand.

A knife.

"But then I heard footsteps, and I ran back into my room, thinking it might be Samuel Rigby. I didn't know who it was until I heard you scream."

"Samuel Rigby," I said softly, mostly to myself. "He suspected you."

"He knows the castle better than a lot of the people who live in it," she said. "He discovered which room was mine and knew I had access to the ruined wing no one else ever entered. He didn't have any evidence, but he made it clear he was watching me."

I shook my head. "Then why did you tell Gordon I was up there?"

"He found me at the base of the stairs," she said. "Waiting for you."

Waiting to attack me.

Hester would have done it that night when I made it back down the stairs. Had Gordon not interrupted her, I would have been ambushed.

"As well as I know the ruined area, I didn't want to chance it without a proper light," she said. "And I knew you were running in the other direction. So, I went to meet you. But I was interrupted."

She moved towards me again, and this time, I took a step backwards.

We were isolated out here. I'd been so fooled by Hester's tears since Alastair's death that I'd wandered into the middle of nowhere alone with her. I'd put myself in serious danger without much of a second thought.

Though, I carefully brushed my arm across my coat and was grateful for the bulge in my pocket. Luckily, I'd had at least one second thought.

Hester knew the castle well. She had lived and worked there for years. She likely knew the grounds just as well. If it came to a foot chase, she would outrun me. And there would be nowhere for me to hide.

"Why did you do it?" I asked.

"I told you," Hester snarled. "You knew too much."

"No." I shook my head. "I'm not asking why you've targeted me. I mean why Alastair?"

Even through the mud on her face, I could see her expression shift. The anger in her eyes changed to sadness, and I wondered whether her tears in the days after his murder hadn't been real on some level. She sniffled.

"Alastair and I were in love," she said, her voice thick. "For a long time, we met in the ruins behind my room. Alastair wanted to be with me. He told me."

"You two were seeing each other in secret?" I asked.

Hester wavered. "It was difficult. Alastair's family—his mother, especially—had expectations, and Alastair was afraid of not meeting them. So, we were waiting for the right time to announce our love."

"How long did this go on?" I asked.

Hester puffed out her chest like she was proud of herself. "Since the day I started working for his family. Our feelings were undeniable."

In that time, how many other women had been lead by Alastair to believe he loved them? He'd broken the heart of Samuel Rigby's daughter, Jenny. According to the admission of both of his parents, he had flirted with almost every woman he ever came into contact with.

So, were his feelings for Hester real or, on her end, imagined?

"In all your time together he never spoke of marriage?"

Even in the darkness, I could see her raise her upper lip. "Things were complicated, I told you. We were planning to run away together. Alastair told me that once he became less dependent on his family for financial support, we would leave the castle and be together. He loved me."

"If he loved you, then why did you kill him?"

"Because of you!" she screamed, charging towards me.

I stumbled out of the way, narrowly missing being tackled by her, and caught myself on a tree trunk.

Hester spun around, her chest rising and falling rapidly. Her eyes were open wide enough that I could see the whites. She looked like a wild animal. "He told me last week that his mother didn't want him to wait any longer. She wanted him to settle down with a lady from a respectable family. He explained that he could never marry a maid in his parents' household. If we were together, he would have to forsake his entire family, and he wasn't ready for that. He couldn't do it. He said he hoped I could understand. And I did. I understood perfectly."

Hester lifted the knife and twisted it in her hand, staring at the blade. "I understood that he had been manipulated."

"What?" I asked, not following. "Don't you mean he manipulated you?"

She shook her head. "No, Alastair was himself with me. His true self. It was with everyone else that he lied. But when we were together, even though it had to be secret, he told me the truth. I knew him like no one else did."

"Then why did he end his relationship with you?" I asked, hoping to break Hester out of whatever kind of hold Alastair had over her.

"Because of you," she said again through gritted teeth. "His parents were pushing him to make a match, and he went along with it. He would have done anything to make them happy."

"Why kill Alastair, then? Why not his parents? Or me?"

Hester reached up and pulled at her hair, tugging until I thought she would pull it out. She paced back and forth, moving like a caged animal. "Because there always would have been someone else. Another woman. Another person to please. And I would always be a servant."

Hester was insane.

That would have been true regardless, considering she'd murdered an innocent man, but watching her pace in the woods, her face coated in drying mud and wearing a stained white dress, I knew she was a madwoman. Truly.

She was not capable of rational thought. I couldn't fathom how she had seemed so normal to me before this moment.

"If I wanted Alastair to be mine forever, then I had to kill him. I had to make sure his soul would be bound to mine, and death was the only way to do that," she said, shaking her head and waving the knife around erratically.

Then, suddenly, she stilled.

After so much movement, seeing her go perfectly still made my blood run cold.

She slowly looked up at me, her red hair an angry halo around her face, and she raised the knife. "And then the beautiful Miss Alice Beckingham arrived."

Hester growled, sounding more animal than human. "Alastair smiled at you and fawned over you, and you didn't even care. I could tell from the moment you arrived that you would never love him the way I did," she said. "He would have been miserable in a match with you. So, I saved him from that fate."

I raised my eyebrows. "You saved him?"

She nodded slowly, her eyes pinned on me. "I saved him from the expectations of his family. Now, he only has to wait for me to meet him on the other side."

"You still love him?" It was part question, part statement. "Then why dress up as the weeping woman in white?"

Hester tilted her head to the side and shook her head. "What are you saying?"

"Your costume," I said, waving an arm at her flowing dress. "Why did you pretend to be the woman from the legend?"

"I'm not pretending," Hester hissed. "I am the weeping woman."

She twirled in a quick circle, the knife held above her head, before she stopped and pointed the blade at me. We were still several paces apart, but it was closer than I was comfortable with.

"Didn't you listen to the story, Miss Alice?" she asked. "The weeping woman lives in the castle forever. She and her lover spend eternity together."

I wanted to ask whether Hester had listened to the story before. Because her version was not at all how Samuel Rigby explained it.

"People will talk about me and Alastair for centuries," she whispered, placing one hand over her heart and looking up at the sky. "They will remember our love story for ages."

Pity washed over me all at once.

Hester was sick. Sick and confused. Her heart and mind had been broken, and she needed help.

In an instant, she slashed the knife out in my direction, her eyes wide and wild again. "I had to stop you before you told anyone about the dress. I knew you were in my room, touching my things. My journal. I had to stop you."

Hester knew I went to the ruined part of the castle. She knew I found the dress and the ring and the door to her room. She had no idea that I had thought all of those things were evidence against someone else. She had no idea that I suspected Samuel Rigby of the crime.

"I couldn't let you tell anyone," she said. "Not until I was ready."

"Ready for what?" I asked.

She looked at me and smiled, her teeth shining in the moonlight. "Ready to join my beloved."

Before I could really process what she'd said, Hester hurled herself at me.

Once again, I avoided being tackled, but I was not as lucky when it came to the knife. She slashed out at me, dragging the blade across my sleeve and slicing open my forearm.

I felt warm blood dripping down my arm immediately and hugged my arm to my chest.

"You don't have to do this, Hester," I said, holding up my other hand in surrender. "No one else needs to die."

"Yes, they do," she said, charging at me again.

This time, I was ready.

I slipped my hand into my coat pocket and pulled out the antique gun I'd grabbed from the display case on my way out of the castle. Little had I known that first day when Charles Barry drew my attention to Lord Drummond's antique weapon collection, how badly I would soon have need of the means to defend myself.

I held the gun up.

Hester's eyes went wide when she saw it, and she dove for the ground just as I pulled the trigger.

The shot rang out, a puff of smoke shooting into the air. Wood shards from the tree behind Hester exploded.

I hadn't been sure the weapon was loaded. As Hester rolled across the ground, trying to get back to her feet, I realized how bad things could have been had it not.

She jumped up, and I leveled the gun at her chest. "Don't make me shoot, Hester. I don't want to kill you."

Her hair had twigs and grass tangled in it, and the dried mud on her face had started flaking off, leaving bits of pale white skin peeking through.

Unexpectedly, she dropped her knife and ran past me into the woods.

The last thing I saw was a flutter of white dress disappearing into the tree line.

17

My run back to the castle was a blur. By the time I got there, my coat was snagged and torn and the blood from the slash on my arm had soaked through my sleeve and spread to my skirt. I looked half-dead.

The first floor was still dark and quiet, so I ran up the stairs and down the second-floor hallway. I went directly to my mother's room.

I knocked once, but then quickly pulled the door open and moved inside.

My mother gasped as she sat up in bed, hugging the sheets around her chest. When she saw it was me, she ran a hand across her forehead.

"Alice, you frightened me." Then, she looked at me. The room was dark, but the sound of my heavy breathing filled the space. "Are you all right?"

"It was the maid," I gasped. "Hester killed Alastair. She cut my arm. She is in the woods."

My mother slid to the side of her bed, lit the candle

on the bedside table, and walked over to me. There was no panic or fear in her face. She didn't look startled or surprised. She simply looked determined.

"Where is she?" she asked, grabbing my arm, wincing only slightly when she pulled back the sleeve and saw the cut.

I was relieved at how shallow the gash was. The way it burned, I'd expected it to be more severe.

"She ran into the woods just beyond the stables. I don't know where she went after that. I ran back to the castle."

"What were you doing out—?" she started before shaking her head. "We need to send for a doctor and alert the police."

Grabbing onto my uninjured arm, she pulled me into the hallway toward Lady Drummond's room. Lord Drummond answered the door quickly as though he had been standing on the other side waiting for this. When I looked past him into the room, I could see the lights were still on. No one had been sleeping.

My mother explained the snatches of story I'd offered her, and Lady Drummond clapped her hands over her mouth.

"Hester?" She turned to me, saw my arm, and then gasped again. "We have to send for a doctor."

"I'll take care of it," Lord Drummond said. "But first, I'll lock the downstairs doors."

"Oh, yes," Lady Drummond said, looking around frantically. "Yes, lock the doors."

Gordon's bedroom door opened a few doors down, and I saw his auburn hair stick out around the frame. "What is going on?"

His mother gave him only the barest information, which caused him to turn to me, wide-eyed, before he was sent to assist his father.

One by one, the doors in the hallway opened, everyone once again awakened by a disturbance in the corridor. Vivian Barry took one look at my arm and led me immediately to the nearest washroom for fresh water and towels. I would never have suspected it, but she had a great deal of common sense in such matters. Soon my arm was cleaned, bandaged, and feeling much better.

After my injury had been seen to, I drifted downstairs to find everyone had gathered in the largest sitting room. Because of the chill in the air, we all ringed the fireplace, although the warm flames had long burned away to smoldering embers. While we sat in the flickering lamplight awaited the arrival of the doctor, and more urgently, the police, I looked at the faces gathered around me. It struck me that our party looked eerily similar to the night when Alastair Drummond had been killed. We had all collected in the same spot then, too. Only a great deal had happened since.

Nobody seemed eager to break the somber silence, until Samuel Rigby spoke up from where he stood in the open doorway of the sitting room. "I should have told everyone of my suspicions against that young maid. It was wrong to keep them quiet."

"You didn't know," I said, trying to ease his conscience. I was sure he would feel better if he knew I had suspected him of the crime.

He smoothed down his mustache with two fingers and pulled his dressing gown tighter around his middle, the legs of his striped pajamas peeking out of the bottom.

"I had no proof, but the position of the maid's room next to the unused portion of the castle gave her the best access to Alastair's room, since it was positioned just across from the door that opened onto the stairway. I posited that she could have used the ruined passageway on the night of the murder to get down to Alastair's room without anyone seeing. After stabbing him repeatedly and leaving him for dead, she could have exited his room through his window, clambering down the tree along the outer wall, before climbing back into the castle through the kitchen window. Then, while everyone's attention was at the other end of the hallway where the dying Alastair had staggered out from his room seeking help, she could have come up the back staircase and returned to her room without anyone seeing her."

"That is likely what happened," I said. "But again, you had no proof, Mr. Rigby."

He pressed his lips together, shaking his head, and I knew I would not be able to dissuade him of his responsibility in my injury.

"I never would have suspected Hester," Lady Drummond admitted. "I knew the girl had a fancy for Alastair, but many of the maids did. He was a very handsome boy." Her voice cracked, and she cleared her throat to continue. "But I didn't think she had any delusions of being his wife. Had I known, I would have dismissed her at once."

We all fell silent again, each lost in our own ponderings.

THE SUN HAD NOT YET RISEN when a pair of policemen

arrived at the castle, coming only minutes behind the doctor who had been sent for. Both the police and the doctor were the same men who had been to the castle only a few nights before, after the death of Alastair. It was strange how similarly events had repeated themselves, only this time at least no one had died.

After a quick examination by the elderly doctor, who swiftly pronounced me fit, my private interview with the police was brief. I explained all that happened the night before, concluding with how I had narrowly escaped with my life before my would-be murderer had made her escape.

Upon taking their leave, the police assured Lord and Lady Drummond, as well as the rest of us, that a search for the dangerous maid would begin immediately.

After that, all any of us could do was wait.

THE CASTLE INHABITANTS did not have long to await events. Shortly after sunrise, word reached us that the young maid, Hester, had been found. Or rather, her body was found, floating in a lake at the edge of the estate. To all appearances, she had taken her own life, rather than face whatever lay ahead.

In one of Hester's pockets, an object was found – a heavy ring, sized for a man, with Alastair Drummond's initials etched across the surface. Whether it had been given to the girl as a gift or stolen by her was impossible to know.

Lord and Lady Drummond received the news somberly. As for me, I was too numbed by my recent ordeal to feel anything but sadness at the tragedy that had been Hester's short and confused life.

Weariness weighing on me after the long night I had experienced, I sought solitude. I found my way to the sitting room and took the chair closest to the fire so that I could stare into the flames. I'd changed out of my ripped, ruined clothes from the night before and into a pair of silk pajamas with a dressing gown over the top. It wasn't appropriate clothing for roaming the castle by daylight, but I was in no mood to care about appearances.

I hadn't slept, and now my exhaustion crept over me like frost spreading over the ground. I leaned back in the chair and rested my hands over my stomach.

"You were determined to prove you weren't the murderer, weren't you?"

I looked up to see Gordon standing next to my chair, his hands in his pockets, a thick vest pulled over his long-sleeved shirt.

"Is that why you think I wanted to unmask Alastair's killer?" I asked.

He smiled sadly. "I'm not sure why else you would care so much."

"Call it curiosity."

"I call it stupidity," he said, sitting down in the chair next to me. "You could have been killed."

I wanted to ask him why it was that he cared so much, but I kept that question to myself. "But I wasn't."

Gordon ran a hand through his auburn hair. The flames brought out even more of the red in it. "I'm still sorry I accused you."

"Please don't apologize again," I said in all sincerity. "I have forgiven you."

"That is well, but it may be awhile before I forgive myself."

I looked at him out of the corner of my eye. "I wouldn't have taken you to be the remorseful type."

"I'm not usually," he admitted. "Though, I will feel even worse if my blunder keeps us from remaining friends."

I gasped, and Gordon looked at me, alarmed, before he realized I was teasing. He rolled his eyes, and I laughed.

"I also wouldn't have taken you for the friendly type," I said.

Gordon sighed and pressed his hands onto his knees as he stood up. "I stand by what I said the day I met you, Alice Beckingham. You are far more interesting than the people around you. And that is the kind of person I'd like to be friends with."

He started to walk away, and I called after him. "Fine. We can be friends."

His mouth turned up in a smile on one side. "Are there any conditions?"

"Yes. The next time we meet, you'll have to come to London," I said. "I'm not returning to Scotland for a long while."

He shook his head and walked away, but before he left the room, I thought I heard him say we had a deal.

18

By midday, Sherborne Sharp had left the castle.

For a moment, I was surprised he'd chosen to slip away without so much as a farewell, but then again, given that he was a thief, sneaking away seemed to be his specialty.

It seemed unbelievable to me that only a few short days before, finding the handsome Sherborne nosing through my mother's jewels had been the most shocking thing I'd seen. Since then, I'd witnessed a violent death, solved a murder, and nearly been murdered myself. In the face of all of that, a small theft hardly warranted a footnote.

I did feel a small amount of guilt, though, when thinking about the wealthy acquaintances Sherborne would go on to victimize. Because although he swore to me his attempt to swipe my mother's jewels was his first dalliance with thievery, I didn't believe him for a moment. He'd done it many times before and would certainly continue to. Perhaps, I'd have the honor of catching him

in the act again one day. I seemed to recall hearing that
he lived in London, after all, so it was not too farfetched
to imagine another meeting in our future.

Vivian and Charles Barry left soon after.

When the house was still reeling after the news of
Hester's apparent suicide, I'd seen Vivian pull Samuel
Rigby aside for what appeared to be a serious chat. At the
end of it, she lowered her head, and he patted her arm
affectionately. They didn't speak to one another again for
the rest of the morning, and when the Barry siblings left,
Vivian refused to look in Samuel's direction.

I could only guess at what they had discussed, but my
instincts told me Vivian was leaving with a hint of a
broken heart.

Charles only seemed relieved. For the first time all
week, he was smiling from ear to ear as they loaded their
things into the car and headed for the train station.

I wanted to leave the same day, as well. However, tech-
nically, we were still ahead of schedule. Our train didn't
depart until the morning, and my mother insisted that it
would be more trouble than it was worth to change our
tickets now and arrange for early transport home. So, we
stayed another night.

Samuel Rigby, too, hadn't planned to leave until the
next morning. And after ensuring his stay would not be a
burden to the still mourning family, he decided to stay
another night, as well. Though, rather than entertain
everyone with stories and tales, he chose to retire early
and read a book in his room.

Based on how quiet the castle was after dinner, it
seemed everyone was in need of alone time.

Lord and Lady Drummond went up to their rooms,

Gordon set himself up with a book and a cup of tea in the library, and my mother pulled out her stationery to write a letter each to Catherine and Rose, explaining the events of the week.

"You reminded me a bit of Rose this week," my mother said in the midst of writing her letter.

"Really?" I asked.

She nodded. "Continue in this way and Achilles and Rose may persuade you to join their agency as another private detective."

"Do you really think so?" I asked.

She narrowed her eyes and then smiled. "No. Because you aren't going to run away to San Francisco and leave your mother behind, are you?"

I had no idea of my plans or where I would be headed, but simply to comfort my mother, I leaned over and hugged her arm. "Of course not, Mama."

She smiled contentedly and went back to writing her letter while I dozed on the sofa, allowing the exhaustion to overtake me for the first time all week.

When my mother finished writing, she tapped me on the shoulder. "We should go say goodbye to the Drummonds."

I groaned, lifting my head. "Won't we see them in the morning?"

"Yes, but it will be early," she said. "We should say a proper goodbye now."

I tried to argue, but only weakly. My mother had an iron will when it came to these things, and I knew I would not persuade her. So I found myself mere minutes later knocking on Lady Drummond's door.

Unlike the last time I'd been in that room, the lights

were on this time and the curtains were opened, allowing the last rays of sunlight to wash across the stone floor. Lady Drummond was sitting up in bed, a tray of food across her lap. Her husband was seated in a chair beside the bed.

"Forgive us for missing dinner," Lady Drummond said. "We weren't quite feeling up to it."

"I don't think any of us were. You didn't miss much in the way of conversation," my mother said.

We spoke briefly of what the couple planned to do once all of their guests were finally gone.

"Mourn, I suppose, and make funeral arrangements," Lady Drummond said. "I know we have been grieving for several days now, but it will be different when the house is empty and it is just the three of us rather than the four of us."

"It will be hard," my mother said, laying a hand over her friend's. "But you will all get through it."

"We have to," Lord Drummond said with a frown.

"And if it is not cruel of me to say so, we have a fine example for how to survive something of this nature and come out of it strong, thanks to the Beckinghams." Lady Drummond smiled at my mother and then at me, her eyes going glassy with tears. "I did not know you then, but I read about your Edward in the paper, and I thought about his poor family all the time."

At that, my mother released a single sob and dabbed at her eyes. "You may have been the only one. Many were not kind to us, after the damage to our family's reputation."

My cheeks warmed at the thought. I still had not

quite come to terms with my brother having been a murderer, it seemed.

Lady Drummond shook her head. "A mother cannot help but love her children. Even if they do things we do not like or condone, they are still our children. And when I read that Edward had been ordered killed in prison by a man on the outside, all I could do was think of his family."

"What?"

Everyone stopped talking and turned to me. I stared back at them, forehead wrinkled.

"Edward was ordered to be killed?" I asked.

Lady Drummond's eyes widened as she looked from me to my mother and back again. "I'm so sorry. Is that just a rumor? Have I revealed myself as a silly gossip?"

"No, no," my mother assured her, patting her friend's hand and then turning to me. "I suppose we may have shielded Alice from some of the finer points of Edward's death. She was younger then, and she had already been through so much."

"Why did they want him dead?" I asked.

I remembered hearing that Edward had been killed. When the information was told to me, he had died in a prison fight. Someone might have targeted him, but it was not a planned killing. Just a random brawl.

"We don't know," my mother said. "And it may just be a rumor, but there were whispers amongst the police at the time that Edward knew too much. He had information about a high-level criminal, and that criminal did not want it getting out. So, he was silenced."

I let the information sink in, trying to rework my memories around it.

"Does Catherine know?" I asked.

My mother shrugged. "We didn't talk about it, Alice. Perhaps, we should have, but it was difficult. None of us wanted to discuss anything that wasn't necessary. So, beyond the simple fact that he had been killed and we needed to plan a funeral, we left the subject alone. If Catherine read anything in the newspapers, she didn't mention it to me."

"I'm sorry," Lady Drummond said, laying a hand over her face. "I didn't mean to bring up any bad memories. I am just not thinking clearly right now."

"Please don't worry," I told her. "I'm glad to know this information. I wish I'd known it from the start."

My mother lowered her head, looking slightly embarrassed, but it had not been my intention to shame her. I smiled, hoping she would realize that.

"You have enough to worry about without worrying that you've somehow hurt my feelings," I said. "Believe me, I will be fine."

"You proved that this week," Lord Drummond said. "Without your bravery, we might not have discovered who the killer was. We might have carried on letting her work in our home and live under our roof."

The thought sent a shiver down my spine, and based on the expression on Lady Drummond's face, it was clearly a distasteful thought to her, as well.

"It may have been less bravery and more stupidity," I said, stealing a line from Gordon. "Though, it worked out well for me."

"And let it be the only time," my mother warned, eyebrows raised.

Lady Drummond laughed, and the sound seemed to

even surprise her. She pressed a hand to her chest and shook her head. "This is the first time I've done that since..."

My mother's lower lip trembled as she laid a hand on Lady Drummond's shoulder. "And it won't be the last."

19

The room was dark and damp, and the smell of it tickled my nose. Each breath was swampy and thick, and I felt like I was suffocating.

I didn't know where I was, and when I tried to open my mouth to say something, no sound came out.

Then, I tried to lift my arms to bang on the wall, but they wouldn't move. Neither would my feet. I was frozen.

Suddenly, the wall in front of me molded and expanded, and there was a door. I strained to walk towards it, trying to get out, but before I could it opened.

And in walked Edward.

My heart stopped.

He looked just like he did the last time I saw him—dark hair, blue eyes, square chin—except instead of his fine clothes, he was in a gray prison jumpsuit. His hands were shackled together with a loose chain between them, and his head was down. He didn't see me.

I tried to yell at him, tried to capture his attention, but

my body was immobile. All I could do was watch as he walked.

The room seemed to lengthen and expand in every direction because Edward was moving, but he wasn't getting any closer to me. I prayed for him to look up and see me, but he kept his head down.

Then, a figure appeared behind him.

Not even a figure. Just a shadow. A man made of darkness who moved behind him and raised his arm.

I knew what was going to happen before it did, and I tried to cry out.

The man brought his arm down, and Edward fell. As he hit the ground, my body suddenly became unstuck, and I dove forward to catch him.

I WOKE up just as I hit the prison floor, jolting up in bed, my mouth open in a silent scream. There was sweat across my forehead and my palms, and I was shaking all over.

It took me a few minutes to slow my racing heartbeat. Then I lay still, gathering my thoughts.

I had told my mother and the Drummonds that the new information about Edward's death hadn't disturbed me, but ever since learning the news, it was all I could think about. I had been replaying every conversation from that period of time, every snippet of discussion I'd managed to overhear while standing outside doors and looking disinterested as others spoke.

One thing came back to me again and again: Rose had mentioned a man called the Chess Master once.

I couldn't remember anything about the conversation, but I remembered the name and the look on her face when she'd said it. There was fear there. Fear associated with this unknown man, and I couldn't shake the feeling that he had something to do with Edward's murder.

Rose had never liked to talk about Edward much. I could understand why. She was the one who discovered he was the murderer of a mutual acquaintance, and he'd tried to kill her, too, in the end. It was an uncomfortable subject for anyone.

However, now I had to wonder whether Rose hadn't stayed quiet about Edward's death for her own safety. Or to protect someone else. The Chess Master, perhaps?

I rolled out of bed and paced the floors. My nap in the sitting room had left me unable to sleep through the rest of the night, and I couldn't wait until dawn. Until we would board the train and get back to London. To home.

Once there, I was going to answer all of the questions I'd been too young to ask when Edward died.

I would write to Rose, of course. Now that I was older she might be more willing to tell me the truth. Any scrap of information I could gather from her would be useful. However, she was so far away. Though I had vowed during this investigation to work alone, it would be nice to have someone closer to home who could assist me next time.

Sherborne Sharp appeared in my mind and wouldn't leave.

As much as I abhorred his particular skill set, it could really come in handy if there arose a need for sneaking and stealing. Plus, he was one of the few people I had information on that I could use for blackmail. My knowledge of his penchant for snatching valuables from the wealthy might be enough to encourage him to help me when and if I ever needed it.

So, I would look him up as soon as we returned to London. With a name like Sherborne Sharp, he couldn't be too difficult to find...

When I next looked out my window, the sky was purple and dark blue, beginning to color with the early morning light. I couldn't resist a final walk on the grounds. So, I threw on my dressing gown, slipped into a pair of shoes, and walked through the still sleeping house to the front doors.

I followed the front path for a few paces before veering away and cutting across the grass. Morning dew gathered on my shoes and splattered against my ankles, but I kept walking until I reached the hill between the castle and the stables. Once there, I turned in a circle, admiring the view from up high.

The grass rolled out in soft hills like the waves of the ocean, and orange and yellow streaked across the sky like scratches in the clouds. The countryside really was beautiful.

Though, when I turned towards the castle and the trees beyond, an eerie feeling came over me.

An early morning fog had moved in, covering the ground and stretching up the sides of the stone walls like climbing ivy, but I knew that wasn't what had unsettled me.

I pulled my dressing gown tighter around my shoulders and began the trek back to the castle to pack. My mother and I would be leaving soon, heading to the train station before breakfast even. And while I was excited, a finger of dread scratched down my neck at the thought of going home.

The ghosts of Druiminn Castle that had stolen my sleep for the last week had proven to be nothing but flesh and blood. There were no more dangers left lurking in the castle or the grounds to harm me.

No, what haunted me now were the unsettled ghosts of my own family's past and the bearing they would have on my future.

~

Continue following the mysterious adventures of Alice Beckingham in
"Murder in the Evening."

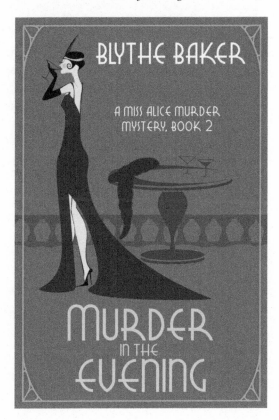

BLYTHE BAKER

A MISS ALICE MURDER
MYSTERY, BOOK 2

MURDER
IN THE
EVENING

ABOUT THE AUTHOR

Blythe Baker is the lead writer behind several popular historical and paranormal mystery series. When Blythe isn't buried under clues, suspects, and motives, she's acting as chauffeur to her children and head groomer to her household of beloved pets. She enjoys walking her dog, lounging in her backyard hammock, and fiddling with graphic design. She also likes binge-watching mystery shows on TV.

To learn more about Blythe, visit her website and sign up for her newsletter at www.blythebaker.com

Made in the USA
Coppell, TX
27 October 2020

40346284R00125